KING DONG

by

Edgar Rider Thingyard

KING DONG

KING DONG

by
Edgar Rider Ragged

HarperCollins*Publishers*

HarperCollins*Publishers*
77–85 Fulham Palace Road,
Hammersmith, London W6 8JB
www.harpercollins.co.uk

Published by HarperCollins*Publishers* 2005
1 3 5 7 9 8 6 4 2

ISBN 0 00 720812 X

Printed and bound in Great Britain by
Clays Ltd, St Ives plc

*This novel is a work of fiction. The names, characters, places
and incidents are products of the author's imagination and are
used fictitiously. Any resemblance to actual events or locales
or persons or primates, living or dead, is entirely coincidental.*

Contents

And the Prophet said, And lo, the Beast looked upon the face of Beauty. And Beauty said unto the Beast, 'You lookin' at me, pal? Stitch that!' And from that day, the Beast was as one dead.

Old Glaswegian proverb

CHAPTER ONE

Rumbuggery on the Lash

In the bustling port of Old Hokum, an old tramp lay against the quay, filthy, neglected, rust-streaked and leaking from every seam.

The ship that loomed above him was in pretty poor shape, too.

Seeing the bobbing approach of a watchman's lantern, the old tramp corked the brown bottle he had been holding to his cracked lips and croaked out a hail. 'Say, friend, what ship is that?'

The watchman was bored, and disposed to be chatty. 'The *Vulture*. Sailing tomorrow.'

The old tramp waved his bottle towards the ship. 'They lookin' for any hands?'

1

The watchman held up his lamp and gazed at the questioner's impressive collection of liver spots and elephant's scrotum wrinkles. 'Now see here, old timer, you don't want to be taken on to that crew, if half of what they say is true.'

The old tramp blinked his rum-reddened eyes and gave a hacking cough. 'What do they say?'

'Why, that the captain of this old rust-bucket has hired it to Carl Deadman, the motion picture producer who's always going off to the most crazy dangerous places he can find to make movies about the world's deadliest critters with scant regard for the lives or sanity of his men, and he's setting off tomorrow for an unknown destination with a highly dangerous cargo and a crew of the worst collection of low-life wharf-rats and plug-ugly desperadoes anyone has ever seen, that's what they say. Why d'you ask?'

'Come to think of it, no idea.' The old tramp picked a louse from his beard. 'How come you gave me such a detailed answer?'

'I think we're supposed to set the scene by providing an opening narrative thread and establishing an atmosphere of mystery and foreboding while at the same time adding a little local colour ...' The watchman broke off. The old tramp was making painful retching noises as his 100 per cent rubbing alcohol diet got the better of him, decorating the quay with a little local colour of his own. Shaking his head, the watchman moved on.

On board the *SS Vulture*, Captain Rumbuggery poured himself another glass of rotgut liquor with a shaking hand, and made a desperate attempt to focus on Carl Deadman. The movie producer was pacing the Captain's insanitary cabin, from wall to rust-streaked wall, furiously chewing on the end of a cheap cigar. A fug of tobacco smoke and alcohol fumes had turned the air into a sickly pale-green mist.

Deadman paused in his perambulation and whirled to face Rumbuggery, slapping his hand down upon the desk. With a drunk's instinct, Rumbuggery lifted his glass from the tabletop just in time to prevent its being knocked over.

'I tell you, Skipper,' growled Deadman, 'sometimes I just can't figure the movie business. I've been out with you on two expeditions to the ends of the Earth. Each time, I've brought back a swell film – and the public, rot them, just don't want to know. I ask you! I put everything into those pictures – blood, sweat tears, even money – and what happens? *An Exciting Movie About a Big Strong Elephant*

3

was box-office poison and *A Thrilling Story About a Big Fierce Lion* didn't even open in the top theatres. How could pictures like that fail?'

Captain Rumbuggery gave a lurid belch. 'I'm flying a kite here,' he slurred, 'y'know, jusht running up the flagpole and sheeing if anyone drops his pantsh – but could the titlesh have anything to do with it?'

'Hogwash!' roared Deadman.

'Plus the fact that your leading men got trampled to death in the firsht picture and eaten in the shecond …'

Deadman waved a hand dismissively. 'I tell you, Skipper, I have it all figured out. My movies have adventure, excitement, spectacle, thrills, danger …'

'And big shtrong elephants and big fierce lionsh …'

'Sure, sure. But they don't have the one thing the public wants. Know what that is?'

'A decent shcript?' hazarded the sozzled Captain. 'Conshistent plot? Compelling dialogue?'

Deadman stared at the old salt. 'What the hell are you talking about, Skipper? No! The public don't care for any of that horse-shit. I'll tell you what they want!' He leaned conspiratorially towards Rumbuggery. 'Sex!'

The Captain stared. 'Shexsh?'

'You heard me! S-e-c-k-s, sex! That's what I need! Sex!'

The Captain fumbled with his belt. 'Well, why didn't you shay?'

'Not now!' snapped Deadman. 'In my movie!'

The Captain rubbed his grizzled chin. 'Well, I don't know ... if it wash artistically valid, and the money wash right ...'

'Holy mackerel! You think the public are gonna pay to see a rummy deadbeat with his pants round his ankles?'

The Captain considered. '*I* would.'

Deadman ignored this. 'No, you old fool, I need a girl. But every flapper I've tried to hire has been interfered with.'

'Well, this *is* New York.' The Captain did a cock-eyed double-take. 'Jusht a cotton-pickin' minute! Are you telling me you're planning to bring a *woman* on board?'

'I sure as hell am! What's wrong with that?'

'What'sh wrong with it?' Captain Rumbuggery spluttered with righteous indignation. 'I'll tell you what'sh wrong with it! Women on board ship are nothing but trouble! Talk about a Jonah. Dischipline goesh to hell! The crew neglect vital dutiesh, such as shteering the ship and shtoking the boilersh and pleasuring their Shkipper. I tell you, Mishter Deadman, I'd shooner have an albatrossh round my neck. I'd sooner have a man-eating tiger on board than a woman!'

Deadman gave the Captain a contemptuous look. 'Oh, pipe down, you old buzzard.'

The blare of an auto-horn from outside caught the movie man's attention. He crossed to the porthole and rubbed at the condensation misting the grimy glass.

A taxi had drawn up on the wharf below. As Deadman watched, a platinum blonde wearing an outrageous amount of cheap fur and fake jewellery stepped out.

Deadman clicked his fingers. 'There's my girl now. Sit tight, Captain. I'll bring her up here and introduce you.' He yanked open the ill-fitting door at the third attempt and headed for the companionway.

By the time he reached the wharf, the argument between his star and the cabbie was already turning the air blue and causing the *Vulture*'s blistered paint to flake off over a wide area.

'Whaddaya mean, wiseguy?' his leading lady demanded as Deadman joined the fray. 'A dollar thoity from Brooklyn? Ya lousy joik, tryn'a rob me.'

'That's the fare, lady.' The cabbie's voice was weary. 'Right there on the meter.'

'I'll give ya meter, ya –'

'Here. Keep the change.' Deadman thrust a five-dollar bill at the cabbie and took his fare by the arm. 'Come along, Darling.'

'Darling?' The cabbie whistled.

'That's my name, ya doity moocher,' the lady replied. 'Ann Darling.'

'Sure it is. And mine's Rudolph Valentino.' The cabbie leered. 'Keep one hand on your wallet with that one, Mac.' He sidestepped to avoid a vicious swipe from Ann's purse and roared off while Deadman restrained his furious star.

A few minutes later, Ann was installed in Captain Rumbuggery's reeking cabin, wrinkling her nose at the foul atmosphere and staring disdainfully at the glass of 90 per cent proof spirit the old sea-dog had considerately poured for her.

'Ann!' Deadman radiated cordiality. 'I'd like you to meet our skipper for the voyage. Captain Rumbuggery – Ann Darling, the leading lady of my new movie.'

Ann gave the Captain a hard-eyed stare and beckoned Deadman closer. 'We're sailing half-way round the world with *him* in charge? The guy's a lush!'

'Only when he's drinking,' Deadman reassured her.

'Oh.' Ann was mollified. 'That's OK, then.' She gave the Captain a winning smile, from sheer force of habit.

Deadman lit another cigar. 'OK, here's the deal. Captain, we sail on the first tide.'

Rumbuggery nodded and tapped the side of his nose. 'Right. Gotcha. Before any shneaky dockside rat getsh to

7

hear about some of the characters we got in the crew – not to mention the *cargo* ...'

Ann's ears pricked up. 'What characters? What cargo?'

Hurriedly, Deadman continued, 'Sure, sure, Skipper. Then you take us to the co-ordinates I've already given you.'

'What's he talking about?' demanded Ann. 'What characters? What's all this about a cargo? What sort of cargo?'

'Yessiree.' Rumbuggery gave Ann a knowing, drunken wink. 'I sure wouldn't want the port authorities to hear about thish cargo.' He gave a phlegmy chuckle which deteriorated into a hacking cough.

'When we get to this latitude,' continued Deadman, 'I'll reveal our destination.'

'I want to hear more about this cargo.'

'I don't like it!' The interruption was sudden and shocking. Rumbuggery's mood, in the way of drunks, had undergone a sudden swing. His voice, powerful enough to summon a favoured fore-mast hand from the fo'c'sle to the Captain's bunk in the teeth of a hurricane, made the solid steel walls vibrate.

'I tell you, it's ashking for trouble.' The Captain's face was a picture of misery. 'You're ashking me to shet sail for an unknown destination ...' The Captain enumerated his points on nicotine-stained fingers. '... on a ship that leaksh like a sieve, carrying a highly dangerous cargo and crewed by the worsht collection of cut-throats and no-goods I ever laid eyesh on – and, worsht of all ...' The Captain's eyes bugged out with indignation. '... with a *woman* on board!'

'Now hold it right there!' Ann shot to her feet, eyes flashing. 'Did you say, "a woman" on board? "A woman" as in "one"? Singular?' She pointed accusingly at Deadman. 'Youse creep, you never told me that!'

'Didn't I?' said Deadman unconvincingly. 'It must have slipped my mind. Does it matter?'

'You betcha it matters!' howled Ann. 'You expect me to spend three months on this hell-ship, being pawed and leered at by a bunch of lecherous deck apes, without even another goil on board? You told me this would be a cruise, with luxurious accommodation on a swell, high-class liner.'

'Maybe I exaggerated a little.'

'I shoulda guessed you were lyin' when youse lips started to move.' Ann fixed Deadman with a furious glare. 'Forget it, buster. Include me out.'

'Well, there's gratitude!' Deadman turned to Rumbuggery. 'Captain, I appeal to you ...'

'No you don't.' Rumbuggery eyed Deadman up and

down, then shook his head decidedly. 'Not one bit. I like lithe young deck-hands with firm, rounded –'

'I *meant*,' grated Deadman, 'I appeal to your sense of fair play.' He pointed accusingly at Ann. 'She hadn't worked for two years. I dragged her out of the gutter…'

'I was *resting*, you joik!'

'Yeah, like you'd been *resting* ever since the talkies came in, and your fans discovered that Ann Darling, the Sweet Maid of Milwaukee, had a voice like a buzz-saw tearing through sheet metal.'

'That ain't fair! I had elly-cue-shun lessons …'

'… till your voice coach threw himself out the window. Get this, doll-face – I hired you because no other producer would touch you with a camera crane.'

'Yeah? Well, no other goil would agree to come on a crazy trip like this.'

'That too,' agreed Deadman. Ann, not sure whether she'd just scored a point or conceded one, gave an injured huff and turned her back on the men.

'While we're on the shubject,' said Captain Rumbuggery, taking yet another liver-dissolving pull at his glass, 'just where the hell are we going?'

Deadman rolled his eyes. 'I told you. I'll spill the beans when we reach the coordinates I gave.'

'No!' Captain Rumbuggery slammed his glass down. Liquid slopped from it and began to eat through the table. 'That'sh not good enough! You exscpect me to take you into uncharted seas and unknown dangersh with a contraband cargo and a woman on board? I won't do it, I tell you!'

'All right, already!' Deadman gave an exasperated sigh. 'I can't tell you everything – there may be spies aboard. But, just to satisfy your curiosity, I'll give you a few hints.'

He bit the end off another cigar. Ann leaned forward, her eyes gleaming with calculation. The Captain tried to focus, and not fall off his chair.

Deadman lit the cigar, puffing hard and rolling it around in the match flame to ensure that the tobacco burnt evenly. He stuck one hand in a waistcoat pocket, took a deep draught of the pungent smoke, and blew three rings which sailed up to join the clouds roiling around beneath the fly-specked ceiling.

Lowering the cigar, he carefully removed a flake of tobacco from his bottom lip. Only then did he turn to face the Captain and Ann.

'Tell me,' he said slowly, 'did you ever hear of … Dong?'

CHAPTER TWO

Deadman's Tales

Dong ... Dong ... Dong ... Dong

The sound reverberated around the cabin.

Dong ... Dong ... Dong ... Dong

Deadman stared through the porthole. 'Who is ringing that goddamn bell?'

'Eight bells!' intoned a salt-roughened voice from the deck.

'Twenty hundred hours, ship's time,' explained the Skipper. He staggered to the cabin door, flung it open and bellowed, 'Will you shut up out there! How'sh an old sea-dog to think with that noise going on?'

'Sorry, Skipper.'

Rumbuggery weaved his way back to his seat. 'Did you jusht shay what I thought you said, Mr Deadman?'

'I did,' nodded the producer.

Rumbuggery's eyes flared with shock and fear. Then they flared again as the light from Deadman's smouldering cigar spontaneously combusted with the alcoholic fumes surrounding the Captain. The smell of singed hair joined the cabin's rich mixture of odours, but the Skipper seemed barely to notice it. 'Dong!' he repeated in a quaking voice.

Ann shrugged. 'Is that the name of the island we're goin' to?'

Deadman shook his head and tapped the side of his nose significantly.

Ann let out an impatient sigh. 'Well, if this "Dong" is a poyson, why don't you stop fooling around and tell us who the hell he is?'

The producer shook his head. 'Dong isn't a "who", he's more of a "what".'

'What?'

'Exactly.'

'Exactly what?'

'Exactly. "What".'

Ann's eyes narrowed. 'Deadman, I swear you'll be soon livin' up to your name, if you don't give us some answers *right now*!'

13

Deadman took a long pull on his cigar. 'I'm talking about the legend of Dong.'

Before Ann could explode, Rumbuggery shook his head decisively. 'Dong! Ha! Dong is a will o the wisp, an old sea-farersh' yarn, a tittle-tattle tall tale told by tellers of tittle-tattle tall tales.' There was a pause. 'Er – I jusht shpat my denturesh out – could you passh them back, pleashe? They're jusht there beshide my shcale model of the U Essh Essh *Misshhisshhippi* …'

'A legend?' Using his handkerchief, Deadman did as requested. 'That's what I thought too, Skipper.' He stubbed out his cigar on the ship's cat, which yowled and hid under the Skipper's bunk. Deadman leaned forward conspiratorially. 'A couple of years ago I was in China, filming *A Nice Movie About a Cute Panda* – a guaranteed blockbuster, how the distributors passed on it I'll never know. When I'd finished shooting, I headed south to Hong Kong to board a steamer for home. My boat wasn't due to leave for a couple of days and I had some time to kill. Wandering the gloomy back streets of Kowloon I accidentally by sheer coincidence chanced upon an opium den.'

Ann's eyes widened. 'You stumbled into a real opium den?'

'Stumbled, hell, it took me hours to find … er, yeah, sure, that's right.'

'Opium!' muttered Rumbuggery. 'The power of the dreaded poppy!'

Deadman frowned at the interruption. 'The dreaded poppy?'

'Aye. Dreaded Poppy O'Shea. Two jam jars high, breastsh like Zeppelins and fishts like a longshoreman. She ran the Dragon's Den House of Forbidden Delights and Hand-Wash Laundry in old Singapore. Hell of a woman.'

Deadman sighed. 'Be that as it may …'

'Oh, believe me, son,' rambled the Skipper, 'I know what the dreaded poppy can do to a man. Fall into her armsh and you're seduced – a shlave to her wilful charmsh. Oh, I know, I know, the dreaded poppy can help you to escape from the depressing reality of thish world, but she'll set you on the road to oblivion. Every minute you spend with the dreaded poppy, you flirt with fear and the danger of helplessh addiction leading to rack and ruin and eventually a horrible tortuous death. Aye, many are the helplessh victims of the dreaded poppy. We used to hold a minute'sh silence to remember them on Dreaded Poppy Day.'

Deadman gave the snootered sailor a quelling glance. 'Have you quite finished?'

'Aye.' A smile spread across Rumbuggery's grizzled face. 'Happy daysh, happy daysh.'

Deadman pointedly turned his back on the Skipper. 'I entered the dismal pit,' he continued. 'The only light came from the glowing charcoal braziers that were heating up metal bowls and filling the room with choking brown smoke. I could just make out shadows and silhouettes of wizened creatures lying on cane beds: Malays, Chinamen, Lascars and Westerners – a motley assortment of the dregs of humanity coming together in a haze of drug-induced dreams.'

Ann nodded. 'Yeah, I been to parties like that – back in Hollywood.'

'In the midst of this hell hole I happened to meet an old sea captain who'd also wandered into this den of lost souls. Although, looking at him, he'd obviously wandered into it dozens of times. As we shared a nocturnal pipe or two, he told me a tale that had happened to him some years previously.' Deadman looked around the room before beckoning Ann and Rumbuggery closer. 'One winter's day, this captain set sail from port with his usual load of passengers when a storm sprang up and before he knew it the ship was off course, lost somewhere in the middle of the Indian Ocean.'

Rumbuggery raised a caterpillar of an eyebrow. 'What ship wash thish?'

'The Staten Island Ferry – it was a hell of a storm.'

'It happensh, it happensh,' muttered Rumbuggery.

'When the storm finally blew itself out, they came across a crudely made inflatable rubber dinosaur drifting on the ocean.'

Ann stared. 'An inflatable …?'

'Don't interrupt! On it lay fourteen bodies. All were dead except for one. The captain hauled the unfortunate creature aboard. He, too, was not long for this world and died soon after. But before the end, he told the captain a blood-chilling story – the legend of Dong.'

'Just a minute,' said Ann. 'How could the skipper of the Staten Island Ferry communicate with some native savage?'

'Through a combination of gestures and an old copy of *Savage Native Lingo for Travellers* the captain always carried with him to communicate with passengers from New Jersey. Even so, he only managed to gather that the poor souls on the raft had come from an island where the inhabitants conducted human sacrifices to a terrible beast. He and his companions had put to sea on the dinosaur; unluckily for them they soon ran out of food and water and all died except for the lone survivor. With his story told, the poor devil breathed his last – his final words were, "Dong … Dong".'

'My eye and Betty Martin!' cried Rumbuggery. ''Tis but an invention of a drug-raddled mind. Nobody would believe it but a raving maniac, a half-witted infant – or a Hollywood producer, down on his luck.'

'I *didn't* believe it,' replied Deadman, ignoring the slur, 'until the captain gave me this …' He reached into his jacket pocket and pulled out a sea-stained, weather-beaten piece of parchment. 'The native had drawn a crude picture, of which only this piece survives.'

Deadman opened out the parchment and set it down on the table.

Ann gave a cry of shock. 'Is that what I think it is? OHMIGOD!'

'I told you it was a crude picture.'

'It's enormous! I've never seen anything so big … and believe me I've seen a few.' Involuntarily, Ann licked her lips.

'Thundering typhoonsh! That's impresshive.' Rumbuggery's voice was awed. 'It'sh enough to give a man a shense of inadequacy.'

'Dong,' said Deadman, gravely.

'You are not just whistlin' "Dixie",' said Ann, dreamily.

'And if the rest of the creature is in scale with this …'

18

Deadman tapped the drawing. '... then it must be bigger than anything that's ever been seen before.'

At that moment there was a knocking at the door. A high-pitched, effeminate voice called out, 'Oh, Mr Deadman, duckie, are you there?'

Deadman scrabbled for the picture, hastily folded it, and rammed it back into his pocket.

'I'm coming! Ready or not!' The door was flung open.

Deadman groaned inwardly. 'Hello, Ray.'

The newcomer was a slim man of indeterminate age. He wore slacks of eye-watering, skin-hugging tightness and a flamboyantly frilled shirt. He had melting brown eyes and sensuous lips, and wore his hair tied back.

Ray gave an ingratiating simper. 'Hello, Mr Deadman, hello Captain Rumbuggery. Oooh!' Ray let out a squeal of laughter and clapped his hand across his mouth.

'What is it, Ray?' asked Deadman.

'I just wanted to ask you about Miss Darling's dress for the screen test. Would you like to go with the crushed silk or the eau-de-nil?'

'Why not ask her?' said Deadman. He beckoned Ann over to make the introductions. 'I don't believe you two have met.'

'Oh?' Ann eyed Ray with her customary calculation.

'Miss Darling,' gushed Ray, 'how very bona to vada your eek at last. Fantabulosa! *Such* an honour, I'm *such* a fan.'

'Oh!' said Ann again, clearly dismissing Ray from her 'to do' list.

'I thought we'd better see what we can do with your riah ...' Ann gave her hair a self-conscious pat. '... and have a little conflab about your cossies. If we stroll down to my cabin, would you be interested in inspecting my wares?'

Ann gave the camp costumier a dismissive look. 'I shouldn't think so.'

'Ooh, you are awful!' Ray flapped limply at Ann's arm. 'I'll think you'd carry off the raw silk very well. How d'you think she'd look in the raw, Mister Deadman?'

'Ask any casting director in Hollywood,' said Deadman nastily. Ann scowled at him. Ray gave a falsetto giggle.

Ann's eyes narrowed. 'If I throw a stick will you leave?'

'You're such a tease – just my type.'

'I don't think so, fly boy. I got a pair of wings and an undercarriage you ain't never gonna be interested in.'

Ray let out an even higher-pitched squeal of laughter. The Captain's glass shattered in his hand.

'Ooh you're soooo naughty. I'm so looking forward to dressing you. I'll just go and lay on some chiffon ...'

'Sure,' drawled Ann. 'Knock yourself out.'

'… and then I'll come and find you. Don't go away now.'

Ann watched him go with pursed lips. 'Who's the squirt?'

'Ray? He'll be dressing you for the movie,' Deadman told her. 'He's a wizard with a needle and thread. Back in Hollywood they call him Fey Ray.'

'I can imagine. But who says I'm goin' on this cruise to nowhere?'

Deadman smiled the smile of the shark he was. 'Doesn't the sight of Dong make you kinda curious?'

The memory of the crudely drawn picture flickered to the forefront of Ann's mind. 'Maybe,' she admitted. 'But let me get this straight – you're askin' me to spend weeks on a beat-up old ship, the only female on board, with dozens of sailors, gawpin' and lustin' after me and watching my every move? What sort of goil do you think I am?'

'An actress.'

'OK, OK.' She held up her hands. 'Ya persuaded me. But what's this cargo the old seagull keeps yabberin' on about? Contraband, he said.'

'I'm not saying anything.' Deadman glared at the Skipper. 'And neither is he. 'Cause if he doesn't keep quiet, then the authorities might find out what really happens at those fish finger parties he throws.'

21

A guilty, fear-stricken look flickered across Rumbuggery's white-bearded face. 'You can't prove nothin'.'

Ann stood up. "Well if I'm joinin' this crazy ship I need showin' to my suite."

The Skipper stared. 'Suite? Oh, sure, *suite*.'

'Yeah. I gotta powder my nose.'

'Huh?' The Skipper stared at Deadman, who closed off one nostril with his index finger in order to mime snorting up some powdered substance...

Ann stamped her foot. 'I mean I want to take a crap, only I was too ladylike to say so, OK?' She turned her back on Deadman.

'Classy broad,' muttered Deadman under his breath. Raising his voice, he added, 'Skipper, maybe you could get someone to show Miss Darling to her *suite*.'

Rumbuggery staggered to the door and hailed a passing crewman. A young, well-muscled, long-limbed, lithe figure dressed in a tight-fitting sailor suit stepped into the doorway.

Rumbuggery introduced the seaman. 'Roger the cabin boy.'

Ann eyed the creature standing before her. 'Is that his name or an invitation?' She turned to Deadman. 'Things are looking up. Maybe this cockamamie cruise won't be so bad after all.' She gave Roger a full-on dazzling smile. 'Hello there. Come on up to my place – wherever that is. Lead on.' She gave Roger a pat on the backside. 'I'm Ann, but you can call me Darling.' She winked outrageously at Deadman. 'Don't wait up, mother, I'm going outside and I could be some time. If you hear me scream, stay the hell out.'

Deadman and the Captain watched Ann and Roger leave. Rumbuggery's lips were pursed. 'I still shtand by what I shaid – this is a foolhardy mission, based on the word of a mind-ravaged lost soul. Itsh dangerous and no place for a woman. A woman'sh place is in the home, peeling potatoesh, whitewashing the coal cellar and taking spidersh out of the bath.'

Deadman raised an eyebrow. 'I think Miss Darling's place is in a cat's home.'

'I don't think much of women on shipsh.' Rumbuggery took a long pull from his bottle. 'Truth be told, I don't think much of women at all. The love of my life ish thish.' He tapped his bottle. 'And my ship – better than a woman any day.'

'How come?'

'Shipsh never need yet another pair of shoesh. Shipsh never ask if their bow is too wide or if their rigging is

23

sagging. You can rent a ship to others by the day and you can tie up a ship without it ever complainin'!'

Deadman shook his head. A leading lady with the morals of a degenerate baboon, a rum-sodden old sea-dog in command and a dresser more camp than a scout jamboree. He sighed. It was going to be a long voyage …

CHAPTER THREE

A Motley Crew

The ship rang with orders.

'Cast off fore – cast off aft.'

'Aye aye, Skipper.'

'Let go the stays, Mister Decktennis.'

'Ooh, thank you, sir – they were killing me.'

'Ware that bucket, Sloppy.'

'If you insist, Skipper, but I don't think it'll suit me.'

'Avast behind, Mister Hawsehole!'

'Well, there's no need to be personal.'

'Weigh the anchor, Mister Obote.'

'Five and a half tons, sir.'

'That's enough sarcasm from you, Mister Obote. Mister Dogsdinner, clear the harbour and steer sou' sou' east.'

'Sho' sho' thing, Skipper.'

Coughing like a tuberculosis ward, the rickety vessel limped its way towards open water in a haze of black smoke. A spasm of foreboding crossed Captain Rumbuggery's grizzled face. 'And may God have mercy on us all.'

Deadman breezed onto the bridge. 'So we're under way at last, Skipper.'

The Captain gave him an unfriendly look. 'Yes, though I can't say I'm happy to be setting sail on this fool's errand. This is an ill-fated ship with an ill-fated crew. I'm mortally certain there's a curse upon us all.'

'What makes you so sure?'

'An albatross just crapped on my head.' The Captain removed his filthy cap and stared mournfully at the newly deposited guano. 'I'm going below. If anyone wants me, I'll be in an alcoholic stupor.'

Deadman watched the departing captain out of sight and shook his head. The Skipper had the jitters: well, Deadman couldn't exactly blame him. The voyage they had embarked on would be enough to try any man's courage.

Still, there'd be no room on this ship for milksops and weaklings. Deadman squared his shoulders. It was time he checked on the crew.

A Motley Crew

The light faded as the movie man made his way into the bowels of the ship, along dimly-lit corridors whose walls glistened with moisture. The air throbbed with the arthritic beat of the engines; from behind the walls came the furtive scrabbling of rats and the less wholesome sound of off-duty crew members removing each others' gold fillings. Deadman reached the crew's mess. He stepped over the mess, wondering why a bunch of grown men couldn't manage to make it to the can in time. Squaring his shoulders, he flung open the door.

Immediately he stepped back, gagging, as a wave of foetid air, redolent of spoiled gorgonzola, athlete's foot and bus station rest rooms burst over him.

Dabbing at his streaming eyes, Deadman gazed around at the dregs of humanity occupying the stinking fo'c'sle. There was the usual collection of Lascars, mulattos, gimlet-eyed Shellbacks, Ancient Mariners and Flying Dutchmen. In one corner stood a painted savage shaving himself with a harpoon. A shrunken head hung from his waist, tied by its hair. At a rickety table, two old seafaring men – one blind, the other with a wooden leg and a parrot on his shoulder – sang an incomprehensible pirate ditty with the chorus, '*Yo ho ho and a bottle of rum.*'

Deadman raised a hand for quiet. The noises of sailors

carving their initials on whalebone trinkets and each other died away into an ugly, brooding silence.

'Men, I guess you know me. Carl Deadman, movie producer.' Deadman scanned the hard-bitten faces that glowered at him from the dingy recesses of their stinking rat-hole. 'I'm gonna be straight with you. When we reach our destination, the going could be rough. I'm going to need men with guts, men who laugh in the face of death.'

'No probleme zere, m'sieu.' The voice came from a hunted-looking individual wearing a striped shirt, a black beret and a string of onions round his neck. 'Zere is not one of us on zis hell-ship who would not sell 'is life for a shot of rum an' think it a bargain.'

'Is that so?' said Deadman. 'And who might you be, sailor?'

'Jacques-François Peep, formerly of the French Foreign Legion. In ze regiment, I was known as Beau Peep.' The man's eyes clouded with pain. 'I joined ze legion to forget.'

'Forget what?'

' 'Ow do I know? I 'ave forgotten. Zat was ze 'ole point!' The man stiffened, and his face turned pale. 'Wait – now I remembair! I was an accordionist – ze greatest in all France! I 'ad a monkey – 'er name was Sylvia – she danced

28

while I played, oh, 'ow she danced, like a small 'airy angel! But one day when I woke up, ze apartment was empty, Sylvia was gone!

'I searched 'igh and low for 'er, I wandered ze streets of Paree without rest, I could not eat or sleep. Zen – I found 'er. She was with a man 'oo was playing ze barrel-organ.' Jacques-François clenched his fists and his lips became flecked with foam. 'She, 'oo 'ad danced to the music of my accordion, 'ad left me for a *cochon* with an 'urdy-gurdy. *Quelle vulgarité*! In my agony, I cried to 'er – "Sylvie! *Cherie!* For what do you prostitute yourself with zis animal?"

'She turned, she saw me, and she laughed. Zey both laughed! Naturally, for the sake of my honour, I 'ad to shoot zem. Ze judge acquitted me because it was a *crime passionel*. So I joined ze legion, an' aftair ten long years in ze fearful 'eat an' desolation of ze desert, I 'ad forgotten ze 'ole tragic affair, until you forced me to remembair ... and now I shall nevair be free of ze memory – nevair ...' The man's voice choked off. His body shook with uncontrollable sobs.

'There, there, Jacques-François. Don't take on so – you'll get wrinkles.' The cut-glass tones betrayed the speaker as an Englishman of the upper classes. He patted the quivering Frenchman on the shoulder and eyed Deadman censoriously. 'All of us on this ship have a similar tale to tell. Mine involves the Rajah of Ranjipoor, his favourite concubine, a polo stick and a bucket of ghee – I prefer not to talk about it.'

'Yeeesh, that eesh sho.' A small, pop-eyed man with a pronounced Hungarian accent leered up at Deadman. 'Een my cashe, eet wash thee Black Bird ...'

'Ze Czarina of oll the Russias,' contributed a man with a monk's habit, a long filthy beard and the eyes of a maniac.

'Thee seex-fingered man who slew my father,' hissed a leather-doubleted Spaniard. 'And when ah find heem, I weel say to heem –'

'Hello,' chorused every one of that desperate crew in a weary sing-song. 'My name ees Indignant Montoya. You keeled my father. Prepare to die.'

Montoya's bottom lip quivered. 'Well, ah weel!' he said petulantly. 'When ah find heem, ah weel keel heem!'

'Of course you will, my friend.' The speaker sported a scarlet-lined opera cloak and impressive dentistry, particularly in the canine department. 'You see, Mr Deadman? This is a ship of lost souls. Who are we? No one. Where are we sailing? Nowhere. Do we even exist? Who knows?!'

'Right.' Deadman backed slowly away, feeling for the door handle. 'Good. OK. Point taken. I'll – er – catch up with you later, OK? Good, er, fine.'

His questing fingers having at last found the handle, Deadman yanked the door open – and Ann Darling sashayed in.

'Why, Mister Deadman.' Ignoring the sudden silence and the lascivious moans of the crew who, having been without a woman for very nearly two and a half hours, were ready to leer suggestively at anything with legs, Ann favoured the slavering cut-throats with her most beguiling smile. 'Aren't you going to introduce me to your … friends?'

'Well, I … er …' Deadman got no further. Howls of fury and screams of agony indicated that a fight for Ann's favours had already broken out. Knives were drawn, blackjacks and knuckledusters brandished. A nose flew by. The air reverberated with the shrieks of men having their ears bitten off.

Deadman glared at Ann. 'See what you did? I'm going to end up with half my crew murdered before we've cleared Ellis Island.'

'Why,' simpered Ann, 'can I help it if the boys are fighting over li'l ol' *me*?'

'You started this, you finish it, or no movie.'

Ann pouted. 'OK, OK.' She put her thumb and forefinger to her lips and gave a piercing whistle. 'Hey, youse bums, knock it off before I nail your cojones to the wall with my hairgrips!'

There was a sudden shocked silence.

'That's better,' said Ann. 'Now, what's goin' on here?'

The peg-legged cove Deadman had noticed earlier adjusted his parrot and stepped forward with an ingratiating air. 'Well, missy, me an the boys was drawin' lots, all friendly like, to see who'd 'ave first chance to get you into 'is 'ammock, an' Blind Pugh 'ere was palmin' the black spot ...'

'Whaaaaaat?' Ann was furious. 'You were drawing lots for me? What kind of goil do you think I am?'

The parrot cackled. 'Piece of ass! Piece of ass!'

The peg-legged man swiped at the bird, which fluttered away, squawking angrily and shedding feathers. 'You'll 'ave to excuse Cap'n Flint,' he told Ann. 'He meant to say, "pieces of eight". I reckon 'e's a mite confused.'

'I say what I see,' squawked the parrot. 'When I say "ass" I mean "ass"!'

Ann looked the peg-legged man up and down. And then halfway up again. Her eyes widened with concupiscence. 'Say, big boy, what do they call you?'

The rascal leered at his disappointed shipmates. 'They call me Long John Silver, missy.'

'And why do they call you that?'

Long John leaned forward and whispered into Ann's ear.

Anne giggled. 'You don't say? In that case, why don't you come up and see me sometime.'

'Oh, I couldn't be comin' near the officer's cabins, missy.'

'Well then, any time you want me, just whistle. You do know how to whistle, don't you, Johnny? You just put your lips together and … blow.' Ann winked at Silver and swayed towards the door. Deadman, belatedly remembering his manners, opened it and followed Ann through. He closed the door, leaned against it and mopped his brow.

'Well, that's just great.' Deadman glared at Ann, who was examining her nails with an elaborate show of unconcern. 'We've only just set sail and you've already got the crew at each others' throats.'

Ann pouted. 'Can I help it if men find me attractive?' She set off down the corridor, swivelling her hips. A crewman, eyes glued to her oscillating caboose, fell down an open hatchway. A scream of agony echoed from the hold.

Deadman shook his head. This voyage was going to be even longer than he'd thought.

Three weeks later the *Vulture* was anchored off the coast of Africa.

The ship had wheezed its way across the Atlantic, producing as much smoke as a middling-sized iron foundry and twice as much noise. Storms had battered the leaking vessel. Many of the crew had been prostrated by seasickness – and, Deadman suspected, many more by his leading lady. In fact, apart from Deadman himself, the only members of the ship's company who had remained immune to the ravages of the voyage were Captain Rumbuggery (who was too blasted to notice the movement of the ship) and Ann, whose self-obsession was such as to be immune to the whims of a mere ocean.

Now Deadman and Ann were leaning on the rail staring at the palm-lined coast of the Dark Continent and chewing the cud about days past.

'You never did tell me how you got into the crazy world of movie making,' said Deadman.

'I was in Hollywood for a screen test. Afterwards the producer said it would take an Act of Congress to get me into the movies, so I thought what the hell! I've been acting and congressing ever since ...'

Their reverie was interrupted by a high-pitched, effeminate voice. 'There you both are, sweeties.'

'Oh hello Ray, haven't seen you for days.'

'I know, I know,' minced Ray. He turned to Ann. 'I'm sorry I haven't been dancing attendance; my dear, I haven't been feeling myself.' He gave a squeal of a laugh. 'Well, maybe once or twice, to pass the time. I've been laid low, drained, positively *overwhelmed* with mal-de-mer. Still, I'm feeling better now this beastly boat has stopped bouncing up and down in that alarming fashion.' He gave Ann a sly wink. 'And rumour has it, that's not the only thing that's been bouncing up and down.'

'If I want any crap outta you I'll squeeze your head.'

'Oh, bold!' Ray's mouth twisted into a little moue of distaste. 'Anyway, I've been cutting, sewing and embroidering like a thing possessed to get Miss Darling's costumes ready.'

He was interrupted by a hail from the bridge. 'Hi, Deadman! I'm shending in the boatsh to fill up the scuttle-butts.' Captain Rumbuggery waved a half-empty whisky bottle at Ray. 'That crazy fella has used all our drinking water for dyeing hish goddamn costhtumes.'

'Philistine!' Ray gave the Captain a savage glare and minced off, his wobbling derriere attracting almost as much attention from certain members of the ship's company as Ann's.

'Boatsh away!' Captain Rumbuggery turned his

wandering attention back to Ann and Deadman. 'You two want to come along for the ride?'

'Sure!' Deadman waved back, and turned to Ann. 'Coming?'

But Ann had spotted a sun-tanned young deck-hand with oiled skin and rippling muscles. 'I think I'll stay here and take in a little local colour.'

Deadman followed her stare. 'Riiiight. Be sure not to take in too much.'

Fifteen minutes later, three of the ship's boats were pulling in an uncoordinated fashion for the shore.

They had almost reached the surf-line when Sloppy, the ship's cook, stood up and pointed. 'Hey, look at that.'

A rider had burst out of the forest, galloping hell-for-leather along the beach. He was a white man, wearing a battered fedora and carrying a bullwhip coiled in one hand, with which he was belabouring the flanks of his foundered horse, urging it to greater efforts.

Behind him, a war party of black-skinned warriors burst from cover. They were wearing leather loin-cloths and carrying buffalo-hide shields and vicious-looking short spears. They pursued their quarry with dreadful purpose, uttering savage war-cries, brandishing their spears with fearsome intent and thirsting for blood.

The rider stood in his stirrups and waved frantically. 'Hey – you down there! Help! They're gonna kill me!'

CHAPTER FOUR

Bones of Contention

'Pull for shore, men!' cried Deadman. 'Pull till your arms creak and your backs break. We must save that white man from those dreadful savages!'

From behind him, a sulky voice said, 'Well, I don't see why.'

Deadman turned to stare at the speaker.

'As you were, Able Sheaman Obote,' growled Rumbuggery.

'Yes, that's all very well,' said Able Seaman Obote petulantly, 'but, I mean, why automatically assume, because he's a white guy and the black guys are chasing him, that he's the good guy and they're the bad guys?'

'Obote ...'

'It makes me sick. People always make assumptions. I mean, if you saw a bunch of white guys chasing a black guy, you'd think, "Hey, that black guy must have mugged somebody or stolen a purse or something. Let's go and help the white guys catch him," but because he's white and they're black you don't give it any thought, you just go barging in on the side of the honky. It's just emblematic of the institutional, unconscious racism that's fundamentally rooted in every aspect of society. I mean, he could have stolen their cattle and raped their women, maybe even the other way about, but do you ask questions? No, you just –'

At a nod from the Skipper, the coxswain had crept up behind Able Seaman Obote, and now brought a belaying pin down on the dusky sailor's head with a solid *thwack*.

Obote's eyes glazed over. 'QED,' he said, and collapsed.

'Goddamn pinko liberal commie political activisht.' The Skipper kicked the unconscious Obote into the bilges as the boat shot through the surf. 'In oars, men!' he commanded. 'Break out the riflesh!'

As the boat ran up the sand of the beach, eager hands tore at the long wooden boxes that had been loaded from the *Vulture*. The lids flew off, and their contents lay exposed.

There was an awkward silence.

'Ah,' said Deadman. 'I guess Ray must have run out of room to store his costumes and – ah – made some extra room by – ah – dumping the rifles and using the crates …' His voice tailed off.

Rumbuggery made an executive decision. 'Back to the ship, men!'

'But what about the guy on the horse?' demanded Deadman. 'We can't just leave him here to be speared to death by those cannibals.'

'How do you know they're cannibals?' cried Obote, who had just come round. 'Cannibalism is comparatively rare in pre-industrial societies. You just have a negative and stereotypical view of any ethnic group you deem to fall short of the arbitrary standards of your so-called civilization –'

Thwack!

'Well done, coxswain.' The Skipper glared at Deadman. 'I'm not going to washte my men's lives on a futile geshture.' He pointed unsteadily at the oncoming war party. 'What are we shupposed to fight them off with, seashellsh?'

'Wait!' Deadman was examining the flimsy contents of the crates. 'I've got an idea, Skipper. Give me one minute.'

The Skipper sighed. 'One minute. And thish had better be good.'

'Right. You men – with me!' Deadman snatched a double armful of costumes from the crate and led the party he had selected into a nearby stand of trees.

The chase was approaching its climax. The rider had nearly reached the boats when his horse stumbled and fell. He pitched headlong from the saddle and landed, rolling. His mount gave a broken-winded neigh, and expired.

'Come on, man!' cried Rumbuggery.

To the astonishment of the crew, the rider, on picking himself up, stumbled back to the horse and began to fumble with the saddlebags.

'Are you crazy?' demanded the Skipper. 'Get over here or you're a kebab for sure!'

Indeed, the refugee was now within throwing range of the war party. Spears rained around him as he tugged desperately at something caught in the saddlebag beneath the horse. Eventually, whatever it was came free, just as a spear went straight through the man's fedora, knocking it from his head. He turned, a cloth-wrapped parcel in his arms, and stumbled towards the safety of the boats, clutching the bundle to his chest. From the way he was moving, the parcel obviously contained something heavy.

Then he put a hand to his head, looked frantically about, and went back for his hat.

As his hand touched the brim, he was surrounded. The boat crew looked on in helpless horror as the pursuers loomed over the doomed refugee, raising their dreadful, razor-sharp weapons, ready to stab, rend and tear …

'Cooo-eeee!'

Startled, the ebony warriors turned. Emerging from the jungle's edge came a chorus line of the ugliest, hairiest matelots in the *Vulture*'s crew, all wearing rouge on their cheeks, curly blonde wigs, and high-waisted print dresses that revealed far too much of their preternaturally unlovely thighs. Mugging furiously, and making a variety of horrendously cute gestures, they falsettoed:

> *On the good ship sodapop*
> *You can get sick at the toffee shop*
> *And throw up all day*
> *On the sunny beach of Sugarplum Bay …*

The warriors' eyes widened. Their hair stood on end, their knees knocked. They moaned and gibbered with primeval terror.

'Aiiieeeee!' cried one, pointing a quivering finger. 'Shirleey Tempellleee!'

'Shirleey Tempellleee!' echoed the others. 'Aiiieeeee!'

Casting aside their weapons in their panic, the war party turned on its heel and fled back the way it had come, leaving its intended victim sprawled on the sand.

Captain Rumbuggery turned a disapproving glance on Deadman as the latter strolled out of the forest, smoking a cigar and grinning from ear to ear. 'Shirley Temple impersonations? That was a pretty low trick to play on a proud warrior race.'

Deadman's grin grew even wider. 'Don't knock it. It worked.'

Released from the momentary sobriety into which the crisis had thrust him, the Skipper weaved towards the stranger. 'Who the hell are you?'

The dusty figure raised its perforated fedora. 'Indiana Bones. Pleased to meet you.' He passed out.

'Likewishe,' said the Skipper. And followed suit.

Back on the *Vulture*, an impromptu conference took place on the aft deck. Several of the shore party were present; except for those who, following their appearance as the curly-haired moppet of popular movie fame, had already attracted partners from the salacious crew and retired below. Captain Rumbuggery having been lashed into his bunk with an attack of the blue devils,

Deadman took the chair for the interrogation of the fugitive.

'So you're Indiana Bones, intrepid explorer and inveterate tomb-robber. What were you doing to be chased by those guys?'

Indiana Bones waggled his fingers through the holes in his fedora and sighed. 'It took me years to get this hat so sweaty and grungy. Now look at it. I guess I'll have to start all over again.' He took another long pull at the bottle that had earlier been torn from the screaming Skipper's clutching fingers. 'What was I doing? That's a long story ...'

'Then let's have the abridged version. We're in a hurry.' Deadman pointed to the wrapped bundle that Indiana had, despite all blandishments, refused to part with since his rescue. 'For starters, what *is* that thing?'

Indiana gave him a cunning look. 'That's what they were after. I recovered it, at great personal risk, from the Lost Temple of Werarwee.'

'The Temple of Werarwee?'

'Yes – I said it was lost. I risked life, limb and academic credibility to break into the innermost sanctum. It was a deadly game of cat and mouse.' The energetic archaeologist shuddered at the recollection. 'The big round rock that chased me, that was the worst. And the spikes that shot out of the floor and ceiling as the roof came down, that was the worst, too. And the room where the gap between the walls got smaller and smaller, and the rats, and the poison darts, and the revolving blades, and the pit of snakes –'

'But what were you after?' Fey Ray, who had taken an instant and obvious shine to the rugged adventurer, was sitting at Indiana's feet, listening with rapt attention to this preposterous farrago of lies. 'What in the world is so precious that you would risk your body and soul in such an insanely dangerous quest?'

Indiana leered at his audience and slowly unwrapped the parcel in his lap. 'The solid gold knobkerrie of Shaka Zulu.'

There was a spontaneous intake of breath from the onlookers.

'Look at the length of that thing,' murmured one.

'It's solid gold,' breathed another.

'And very knobbly,' gasped a third.

'Lemme see.' Unnoticed, Ann had joined the conference. Indiana looked up to see who had spoken – and pointed like a retriever. An idiotic smile played across his rugged features. His eyes glinted. Ray pouted.

Ann reached for Indiana's treasure. Eyeing her like a wolfhound declaring an interest in a nice, juicy ham-hock, Indiana handed it over.

Ann gasped at the weight of the object. Then, tongue

protruding, she ran her hands over the heavy, golden artefact. With great deliberation, she stroked the long, sturdy shaft. Her eyelids half-closed as she caressed the bulbous shape at the end …

Three men fainted dead away.

Anne purred. 'Hey, this is really something.'

Indiana gazed at her with unbridled lust. 'Do you know what it is?'

'No.' Ann's hands slid over the smooth metal. 'But I could have a damn good guess.'

'It's a ceremonial staff of office derived from a stick with a heavy bulge at the end, used as a war club.'

'Well, I was wrong.' Losing interest immediately, Ann dropped the golden dingus back in Indiana's lap. As he doubled up in agony, she said, 'What time does Sloppy open the cook-house on this banana boat? I'm starving,' and flounced off.

Ray looked at the moaning adventurer with a finely poised mix of revenge, sympathy and opportunism. 'Shall I rub it better?'

Hastily, Indiana shook his head.

Ray gave a petulant shrug. 'Suit yourself.'

Deadman's patience was wearing thin. 'Now see here, Dr Bones, we've all heard of your heroic exploits –'

'Oh, really?' said a familiar voice. 'Let's just get this straight, shall we? This guy claims to be a serious scientist, yet he steals objects of great value from helpless, impoverished indigenous peoples without any regard for their significance or any attempt to record or interpret what he's found, and sells these priceless artefacts for vast sums on the international antiquities market. Now how does that make him a hero, exactly?'

Thwack!

'Well, thank you for that cogent and closely reasoned riposte.' Able Seaman Obote folded up like a deckchair.

'Like I was saying, Dr Bones,' Deadman continued, as if the interruption had never taken place, 'I'm damned if I know what to do with you.'

'Give … me a … ride … to my next … port,' gasped Indiana, rubbing at the affected area. 'I've heard of a fantastic treasure in the Himalayas. There's a one-eyed yellow idol to the north of Kathmandu and its remaining green peeper has got my name on it. If you could just see your way clear to take me to Calcutta …'

'Goddamn it, man!' exploded Deadman. 'I've got a movie to shoot. This isn't an archaeology expedition, and we don't have time for sightseeing trips.' He considered. 'However, there's a strong chance we may have to deal with an ancient and mysterious culture, in which case your expertise may be valuable. What's more, since the second assistant chef ran amok in the galley with a meat-axe the other night and we had to throw him over the side, we're a man short in the kitchen and there's a mountain of potatoes to peel between here and our mysterious destination.'

'Now hold it right there!' Indiana was on his feet, his eyes blazing defiance. 'I have a Master's degree from Oxford and a PhD from Harvard, I'm a member of the Royal Society, the National Academy of Science *and* the Benevolent and Protective Order of Elks, and I'm damned if I'm going to waste my time doing KP for a bunch of lowlife chancers.'

'Or we could leave you for the Zulus.'

Indiana rolled up his sleeves and pulled out his sheath-knife. 'Would you like me to do the carrots as well?'

CHAPTER FIVE

Tall Tales and a Big Whopper

'Hi there, baby.'

Ann gave Indiana a sidelong glance. If she was pleased to see him, she hid it well. 'Are you by any chance talking to me, buster?'

'Well – er – yeah.'

'Then I would be grateful if you would have the coytesy to address me as "Miss Darling", as befits my position of being a lady of class and distinction, ya dumb-ass.'

Indiana backtracked hurriedly. 'Oh, sure, Ann … Miss Darling. Anything you say.'

There was a long pause while Indiana tried to catch Ann's eye and Ann resolutely ignored him. At length, shuffling his feet, Indiana said, 'You doing anything special tonight?'

'Well, I thought I'd take in a movie, and then go down to the Plaza Hotel for supper, and finish up dancing the night away at Radio City Music Hall – what the hell d'ya think I'm gonna do?' snapped Ann. 'I'm gonna eat a pailful of slop and go back to my lousy cabin to read a crummy magazine I've read three times already, like I do every night, that's what.'

'Well, I thought …' Indiana examined the backs of his hands with inordinate interest. 'I thought, maybe, you'd like to stay out here on deck with me and look at the stars.'

Ann gave Indiana the sort of look she usually reserved for weevils she'd found in a ship's biscuit. 'I like my plan better.'

'Well, hello.' A waft of eau-de-Cologne, strong enough to stop a charging rhino in its tracks, announced the arrival of Ray. The effete couturier stood, hands on hips, and eyed Indiana and Ann satirically. 'Beauty and the beast, eh?'

Ann smirked. 'Beauty, eh? Why, thank you, Ray.'

'What makes you think,' drawled Ray contemptuously, 'that "Beauty" referred to you?'

'Blow it out your ears, fancy-pants.' Turning her nose up, Ann high-heeled away across the deck. Indiana watched, entranced, as a member of the ship's company accosted her in an over-familiar manner, and she kneed him in the meat and veg with a force that sent the luckless matelot's glass eye shooting over the starboard rail to splash into the limpid waters of the Indian ocean below.

'Wow,' breathed Indiana. 'That is some woman.'

Ray pouted. 'I don't know what you see in her. Hard-faced baggage. A real train-track woman – she's been laid from coast to coast.' He slipped a more-than-companionable arm across Indiana's shoulders. 'Take it from me, sweetie. Women are poison.' He wrinkled his nose. 'Pooh! Are you still wearing that smelly old leather jacket? Why not let me run you up a new outfit? I could knock up something in your cotton. Or maybe your denim. I could really let myself go in your denims.'

Indiana began to edge away. 'Er … no thanks …'

'Or maybe something softer. How about nylon?' Ray sidled after Indiana, trapping him in a corner of the rail. 'I'm unbelievable in nylons.'

'I bet you are.'

'Or maybe rayon? You haven't lived until you've had rayon.'

'Uuuuurgh,' croaked Indiana.

'Or maybe you'd rather stick to leather.' Ray ran his fingers up and down Indiana's disreputable lapels. 'I like sticking to leather, myself.'

'I'm sure you do.'

'Suede?'

'No, I'm not in the least swayed, honestly.'

'Saucy! Well, I'll think of something. Come down to my cabin and we'll take a gander at your inside leg.'

Indiana glanced downwards at the ocean, briefly wondering whether certain death in its shark-infested waters was a better option than the fate the besotted costumier had in mind for him.

'Hey! Dr Bones!'

Indiana felt himself go weak with relief. Deadman had emerged onto the wing of the bridge two decks above, and was beckoning to him. 'Sorry,' he gabbled, pushing none-too-gently past Ray, 'Mr Deadman wants me. Glad we had this little chat – mustn't keep the boss man waiting.'

'Oh, go on then.' Ray gave a disgruntled wriggle. 'The laddie doth protest too much, methinks. I'll turn you round sooner or later, you'll see.'

'Not while I have my strength,' Indiana muttered under his breath as he took the companionway steps two at a time.

Deadman greeted him at the door to the bridge. 'Well, Dr Bones – Fey Ray seems to have taken quite a shine to you.'

'"Fey" is right.' Indiana pawed frantically at the movie man's sleeve. 'You gotta call him off, Deadman.'

'Funny thing, romance.' Deadman gave Indiana a shrewd look. 'You and Ann, Ray and you. Who's Beauty and who's the Beast? It ain't always safe to make assumptions. I guess, like the song says, beauty is in the eye of the beholder. One thing I do know: when Beauty comes in the door, the Beast starts thinking with his cojones and he's fixin' to wind up with his ass in a sling. Think about it, Indy.' Ignoring Indiana's spluttering attempts to protest his innocence, Deadman continued, 'Anyhow, that's not why I called you up here. We've reached the coordinates I gave the Skipper. Time you all found out where we're headed.'

Indiana followed him into the dog-house where the Skipper was trying to focus his bloodshot eyes on a chart. 'Here we are, Deadman,' he slurred. 'Right where you shaid. 7 degreesh north, 06 degreesh west.'

'What?' Deadman stared at the Skipper. Then he grabbed at the chart. 'You've got it upside down, you old fool.'

The Skipper blinked. 'Sho I have. I wondered why India wash to the south and pointing upwards.'

Rolling his eyes, Deadman spun the chart and jabbed with an index finger. 'This is where we are – 2 degrees south, 90 degrees east.'

'But we're in the middle of nowhere,' protested Indiana.

'Sure, that's what everyone thinks ... but they're wrong.

According to my information, there's an uncharted island just to the south west of here. A mysterious land hidden in a bank of fog which defies meteorological explanation, and which has unaccountably failed to arouse the interest of the hundreds of experienced mariners and explorers who have criss-crossed these waters for centuries and surveyed every inch of the sea-bed.'

'An island?' The Skipper's wandering attention had caught up with Deadman's opening remarks. 'What short of island?'

'This sort.' Deadman took a much-thumbed paper from his inside pocket. He unfolded it and spread it out on the chart table. 'Here it is – Skullandcrossbones Island. That native I told you about – he roughed this out before he died.' He pointed. 'The only approach to the island is through an inadequately charted reef, whose razor-sharp rocks are easily capable of ripping the keel out of any ship foolhardy enough to attempt the passage. Then there's this isthm … itshm … strip of land here, next to this sandy cove.'

'Sandy Cove?' The Skipper gave Deadman a bleary-eyed stare. 'Is he there?'

'What?'

'My old pal Sandy Cove, bo'sun of the *Saucy Mrs*

Truscott out of New Orleansh, used to be a ship-mate of mine.'

'No, I mean this sheltered bay.'

'Shelta'd Bey? The Turkish envoy to Rangoon? I met him in the Ninetiesh.'

'No, no, no, this minor haven.'

'Mina Haven? Lovely girl, Nautch dancer from old Bombay.'

'... this handy landfall ...'

'Andy Landfall? Ish he there ash well? Funny, I thought he wash dead.'

'Oh, it's no good.'

'Noah Goode? Haven't sheen him in yearsh.'

'Look here, Skipper ...'

'Luke Earskipper? Last of the Fighting Earskippers.'

'Skipper!' roared Deadman. 'I'm not reminiscing about old friends of yours. I'm trying to tell you about this lousy island.'

'Lucy Ireland?' The Skipper brooded for a second. 'Nope. Never heard of her.'

Deadman counted to ten very slowly. 'Now, across the end of this coastal plain is a wall.'

Indiana stared. 'A wall?'

'What are you,' grouched Deadman, 'a parrot? Yes, a

55

wall, almost a hundred feet high and as tough as old army boots, a wall built long ago by a lost civilization. It cuts the peninsula off from the rest of the island. All the natives live on the peninsula, and they keep the wall in good repair. They need it.'

'Why?

'Because on the other side of the wall is something terrible, something monstrous, something so goddamn scary that fourteen of the locals put to sea on an inflatable dinosaur rather than face the menace any longer. And the name of that creature is – Dong.'

'Dong? Ha!' said Indiana dismissively. 'Dong is just a superstition. A god, a spirit, a story islanders tell their kids to get them to eat their greens.' He laughed. 'You've fallen for a load of baloney, Deadman.'

The movie man shook his head. 'Oh no, Dr Bones. Dong is far more than that. Not a beast, not a man, but something huge and immensely powerful. Remember that native drawing I showed you, Skipper?'

Rumbuggery blenched. 'That wash Dong?'

'A part of him, at any rate.' Deadman reached into his pocket. 'You want to refresh your memory?'

The Skipper waved the offer away. 'No, I don't want any part of him, thank you very much. I know my limitationsh.'

'According to my information,' continued Deadman, 'Dong lives on the other side of that wall along with many other things that were thought to have perished long ago – monstrous, savage beasts from a former time, beings out of nightmare, creatures the world forgot. Whatever Dong is, he rules the island with a grip of iron.'

'Yesh,' muttered the Skipper, 'he'd need a grip of iron with a –'

'Poppycock!' scoffed Indiana.

'– exactly, with a poppycock that size.'

'Oh, this whole Dong thing may be superstition, I'll grant you,' conceded Deadman. 'But every superstition has a basis in fact. I tell you, there's something on that island that no white man has ever seen.'

'Oh, big deal!' Able Seaman Obote, who was at the helm, stuck his head into the dog-house. 'Of course, nothing exists until some honky has seen it. Like North America, full to bursting with black folks, well, red folks, near enough – but it don't count until some damn Spaniard "discovers" it when he's lookin' for somethin' else, not to mention Africa, crawlin' with peckerwoods in pith helmets, "discoverin'" this lake and "discoverin'" that waterfall when thousands of black folks knowed they were there the whole time, I swear, that makes me so –'

Deadman kicked savagely at the door, which swung shut in Obote's face. A faint cry of 'Oh, by node!' came from the wheelhouse, followed by the thump of an unconscious body hitting the deck.

Indiana folded his arms and favoured Deadman with a disbelieving smile. 'So you're fixing to find this "Dong", whatever it is, and film it?'

'You bet I'm going to film it. It's the subject of my next picture: *A Scary Movie About a Gigantic Dong.*'

Captain Rumbuggery shuddered and grabbed frantically for his whisky. He tilted the bottle and glugged noisily.

Indiana's grin widened. 'This I must see.'

Ann glowered at the camera. 'What do I got to do a screen test for?'

'It's just routine, angel-face.' Deadman's manner was conciliatory. 'I need to see how the light falls on the costume.'

'And that's another thing. We're goin' to a tropical island, right? So what for do I have to get dragged up like Joan of freaking Arc?'

'What's wrong with the costume?' demanded Ray heatedly. 'I *slaved* over that costume.'

'Just look at it – peach, with my complexion! Are you colour blind?'

'Honey, it's a *black and white* movie.'

'Will you two knock it off?' Deadman's voice was weary. 'Can we just get this test done? The light's fading.'

'But it's only mid-afternoon,' protested Ann.

'It's still fading. Now listen, Ann. I want you to be just standing by the rail there, that's it.' Deadman reached for the movie camera he'd set up for the test. 'Now, when I start cranking –'

'Hey! What kind of a goil do you think I am?'

'Cranking!' snapped Deadman. 'Cranking the camera.' He turned the handle that operated the winding mechanism and shutter by way of illustration.

'Oh,' said Ann. 'Yeah. I knew that.'

Deadman gritted his teeth. 'As I was saying, when I crank the camera, I want you to look up. That's it … further … further … and you see something, Ann.' Ann's eyes widened. 'Good. You're amazed. You can't believe it! What you're seeing is terrible – monstrous – obscene – but you can't look away.' Ann's face crumpled with horror. Her mouth worked. Her hands strayed towards her chin. 'That's it! Great reaction! There's nothing you can do, Ann – except scream! Scream till your throat is raw! Scream, Ann! Scream for your life!'

Ann threw her forearm across her eyes, opened her

mouth and screamed – a piercing scream of pure, unadulterated horror. She screamed and screamed and screamed.

Deadman stopped cranking the camera. 'Yeah, that's great, Ann, but I took the shot. You can stop screaming now.'

Ann continued to scream, her terrified eyes fixed on a spot above Deadman's head. He stared at her in puzzlement for a few moments, then turned to follow her appalled gaze. 'Oh, for pity's sake, Skipper,' he yelled, 'go and put some clothes on!'

Rumbuggery stood swaying on the bridge wing, stark naked, his eyes wide, every muscle of his flabby body twitching. 'They're comin' to get me,' he moaned indistinctly, 'all hairy, with eyes and teeth and tentacles, and *green* … aaarrrggghhh!' The Skipper stumbled into the wheelhouse, swatting furiously at things only he could see.

'Looks like the booze has finally got to the old boy.' Deadman shook his head regretfully. 'Oh, well – we'll try another shot, Ann … Ann?'

'Yeah?'

'Where are you?'

'Over here, dummy. Where I was before.'

'I can't see you.'

'That would be on account of the fog.'

'Fog?' Deadman looked around. Ann was right – while he had been talking to the Skipper a dense fog bank had descended on the ship. It lay over the rusty vessel in a cold, clammy mist, reducing visibility to practically zero, blanketing sound.

'Fog!' Deadman was delighted. 'You know what this means?'

'I sure do. My dress is clinging to me like a Latin gigolo, and my hair is all mussed.'

'No, no, no!' Deadman stared frantically into the fog, as if trying to pierce its secrets. 'It means we must be close to Skullandcrossbones Island.'

Ray gave a squeak of alarm. 'Then shouldn't we get those naughty sailors to do whatever it is they do to stop the boat before we crash into it?'

'You're right.' Deadman raised his voice. 'Hey, Skipper!'

A thin wail arose from the wheelhouse. 'Ohgodohgod-ohgodohgod, gerremgerremgerremgerrem*off* ...'

'Oh, never mind. I'll do it myself.' Deadman raised his voice to a stentorian bellow. 'Stop engines!'

The voice of the helmsman echoed the command. 'Stop engines, aye.'

The rumble of the engines died away. The ship ghosted

through the mist, slowing until its bow wave was merely a ripple.

Indiana appeared at Deadman's shoulder. 'What's up?'

'You know that island you think doesn't exist? We just found it.' Deadman listened alertly, straining to catch the faintest sound. He was rewarded: from somewhere in the depths of the mist there came a rhythmic, pounding sound, faint and indistinct at first, but growing louder and clearer moment by moment.

Indiana stared into the mist. 'Is that the pounding of surf on a strangely sinister foreign shore?'

Ray clutched at Indiana's arm. 'Is it the terrible war chant of a hostile tribe, working itself up into a frenzy before forcing us to join it in a barbaric ceremony culminating in an orgy of wanton sexual depravity, with any luck?'

Ann turned to face Deadman. 'Is it the raw, primeval sound of native drums?'

'No.' Deadman turned an astonished face to the others. 'If you listen carefully you'll notice that it's the raw, primeval sound of a native gramophone playing "Is You Is or Is You Ain't My Baby?"'

CHAPTER SIX

Welcome to Dongland

The *Vulture*'s engines once more throbbed into life. On the bridge, Captain Rumbuggery was alternating between guzzling from his ever-present grog bottle, fighting off his unseen demons and peering shorewards through an old brass telescope. 'We'll make for the passage through the reef. Take her in. Full shteam ahead, Mr Krishtian!'

The heavily bandaged helmsman shot him an angry look. 'That's Mr *Obote*, Captain, and I am not a member of any religious group. I believe that organized religion is the opium of the masses, an amalgam of catchpenny shibboleths designed to stop people thinking for themselves –' Obote broke off, staring at the waves breaking on the reef surrounding the island. 'Er ... don't you think we're getting a little close to the reef?'

'I can see the breakersh clear enough in my telescope. We've plenty of leeway. Full shteam ahead.'

'But, Skipper!' protested Obote.

'Mr Krishtian, who is the captain of this vesshel?' roared Rumbuggery. 'The reef ish a long way off. The teleshcope doesn't lie!'

'But ...'

'Is this mutiny, Mr Krishtian? There's no possibility of us hitting –'

CRUNCH!

'– the reef. Shod it.' Rumbuggery peered quizzically at his telescope. 'I could have shworn ...'

'It helps if you hold the damn thing the right way round,' pointed out Obote. 'See what I'm talkin' about? The white folks never listen to the black folks.'

Rumbuggery wasn't listening. 'Don't panic, don't panic! Everything ish under control. Get away from me, you devilsh!' The Captain swatted the air in front of him before putting the bottle to his lips and downing the stomach-destroying contents in one gulp. 'Abandon ship! Women, children and drink-sodden, cantankerous Captains first!' Rumbuggery flung himself out of the wheelhouse and vaulted over the bridge rail. Indiana, Ann, Ray and Deadman watched open-mouthed as the crazed Skipper hit the water below with an almighty splash. In a moment he was surrounded by grey fins, which sliced menacingly through the surface as they spiralled inwards.

Ann shuddered. 'I ain't seen so many sharks in one place since the last agents' convention.'

The water around the struggling Skipper boiled, turning red. There was a threshing of sleek, grey bodies, one drawn-out, agonized scream – then nothing but silence and a small white cap with a black peak bobbing on the empty sea. After a moment, an empty grog bottle broke surface to float alongside it.

Deadman wrung his hands. 'This is terrible! It's appalling!

Indiana nodded sombrely. 'It sure is.'

'What a waste,' said Ann.

'You're right,' wailed Deadman. 'It's a tragedy!'

Ray shivered. 'Don't worry, Mr Deadman. I'm sure the poor old Skipper didn't feel a thing.'

Deadman gawped. 'Who gives a shit? I mean it's a tragedy that I didn't have the camera running!'

The others turned to stare at him.

Deadman spread his hands. 'What?'

The ship continued to grind against the coral reef. The air was filled with the groan of tortured metal.

Obote peered over the bridge rail. 'I hesitate to break in on a deeply meaningful dialogue between my social superiors, but I was wondering whether, before this ship tears itself to pieces on the rocks, anybody feels like giving the order to stop the engines?'

Deadman tore his eyes from the scene of his missed opportunity and screamed at the helmsman: 'Stop engines!'

'I thought you'd never ask.'

The rumble of the engines died away. The grinding noise abated as the ship settled on the coral reef.

'Let go the anchor!' ordered Deadman.

'Oh, now we're firmly aground he wants to let go the anchor. Why does that put me in mind of stable doors and bolting horses?'

'Just do it, Obote, or whatever they call you.'

'They call me *Mister* Obote!' The cross-grained helmsman barked an order. There was a splash followed by the ferocious clatter of the anchor chain rattling through the hawsehole.

Deadman gazed towards the forbidding shoreline of Skullandcrossbones Island with a mixture of excitement, fear and wonder. There, in the distance, lay the beach ... the native village … the great wall, with the brooding cliffs beyond … the amusement park …

Deadman did a double-take. Amusement park?

The space between the village and the wall was filled with bamboo ferris-wheels, rickety wooden roller-coasters and primitive swingboats. Some of these were unfinished, and all looked dilapidated. A tumbledown fence surrounded the park. In the side facing the lagoon was a gate, above which tattered banners wafted forlornly in the breeze. A sign above the gate read:

WELCOME TO DONGLAND

Indiana stared at the unkempt attraction in shocked disbelief. 'Dongland? What the hell is Dongland?'

'Well, we're not going to find out just sitting here looking at it.' Deadman raised his voice and called to Obote. 'We're going ashore. Give the order to break out the boats.'

A villainous-looking crewman with two black ears and a cauliflower eye shambled forward. 'Beggin' yer pardon, sir, be I right in thinkin' it be your intention to go ashore on yonder mysterious an' sinister island.'

'Damn right,' Deadman told him.

'Well, sir, me an' the lads is just a mite concerned about

that, seein' as 'ow your … friend 'ere …' The rascal gave Ray an impertinent leer. '… 'as apparently dumped all our rifles out to make room for 'is frills and furbelows …' The crew, ranged behind him in support, nodded grimly.

Deadman gave them a jaundiced look. 'And I don't suppose any of you have … *private* means of settling disputes among your personal effects?'

The crew shook their heads owlishly.

'Let me rephrase that. I will stop your grog ration with immediate effect unless every man in this ship produces a concealed weapon – *Ray, button your flies, I'm talking about firearms, OK?* – right this minute!'

A blur of movement and outbreak of metallic clicking produced an impressive display of hardware, ranging from ten-inch bowie knives, through Lugers, Smith & Wesson revolvers, Lee Enfield rifles and Thompson sub-machine guns to flamethrowers, field mortars and a 75 mm howitzer.

Deadman gave a wolfish grin. 'I'd say that was adequate for purely defensive armament. To the boats!'

Some time later, two boats pulled away from the *Vulture*, heading to the island. They rode low in the water, weighed down by several large and heavy wooden crates.

'That's the contrary ... contrarrr ... the hookey stuff, isn't it?' said Ann.

Deadman replied with a wink, a grin and a tapping finger on the side of his nose. 'Pull away, boys!' he ordered the boat's crew. 'In, out, in, out ...'

Ann, sitting in the stern, eyed the rippling biceps and straining thighs of the crew as they hauled on the oars. 'In, out,' she echoed dreamily. 'In, out, in, out, in out, in out, inoutinoutinout ...'

The rowing became ragged. Three of the rowers caught crabs and fell backwards off their seats. Deadman glowered. 'Steady on the oars, men.'

'There's one oar too many on this boat,' muttered Ray, 'if you catch my meaning.' Ann shot him a poisonous glance.

The landing party had evidently been spotted from the shore. A crowd of natives had emerged from the rude huts of the village and assembled on the beach. They were waving palm-fronds, items of clothing – anything, it seemed, they could get hold of – beckoning the visitors with welcoming gestures that went beyond enthusiasm into something very like desperation.

'They seem pleased to see us,' said Indiana guardedly.

Ray had been sketching the native costumes: now he lowered his pad, chewed on his pencil, and looked thoughtful. 'There's something queer about those natives.'

Ann curled her lip at Ray. 'You should know.'

'I'm talking about their *clothes*, sweety-pie.' Ray's lips pursed as if sucking a lemon. 'Somebody's mouth is getting too big for her muzzle.'

'Yeah?' snapped Ann. 'Can I borrow your face for a few days while my ass is on vacation?'

Deadman gave a weary sigh. 'Knock it off, you two.'

'She started it,' grumped Ray.

Deadman shook his head. It was obviously a forlorn hope that his star and her dresser were ever going to stop sniping at each other. 'What did you mean, Ray? About the natives?'

Ray gave Ann a triumphant look. 'What I *meant* was, among primitive savages I'd expect more in the way of grass skirts, bone necklaces, capes made of feathers – and less in the way of knee britches, gold earrings and headscarves.'

'Oh, sure,' Obote piped up from the helm in bitter tones. 'Nobody expects to see a brother in an Armani lounge suit; no sir, he just naturally got to dress like he been fitted out by the Garden Supplies department.'

He was interrupted by what sounded like agonized moaning. As his ears adjusted, Deadman realized that what he was hearing was a song, which the welcoming party onshore was belting out with great enthusiasm but a complete lack of regard for rhythm or melody:

'When you wish upon a Dong,
Whether it be short or long,
Anything your Dong desires
Will come to you.
If the Dong is in your dreams,
No size can be too extreme
When you wish upon a Dong
As lovers do ... '

Deadman looked helplessly at his companions. 'Does anybody have the slightest idea what the hell is going on here?' Indiana and Ann shrugged. Ray shook his head. Deadman sighed. 'Well, I guess we'll find out soon enough. Anyway, this is an opportunity for a great shot. Our arrival at Skullandcrossbones Island!' He began to set up the camera. 'I aim to build up the tension through a sense of foreboding.'

'If you say so,' said Ann dismissively. 'Poysonally, I'd make the oidiance noivous by making them wonder what's going to happen.' Ray rolled his eyes.

Deadman pointed. 'Ann, I want you in the prow of the boat.'

71

'You mean the front?'

Deadman gritted his teeth. 'Yes.'

'Well, if you mean "the front",' pouted Ann, 'why not say "the front"? Why give me all that nautical crap?' Brushing against as many sweaty seamen as possible, she made her way to the bow.

'But what about her hair and her make-up?' protested Ray.

'No time for that,' snapped Deadman. 'We've got to get the shot.'

'Well, don't blame me if she looks like the tramp she is.'

Ignoring Ray, Deadman called to Ann: 'OK, sweetheart, I want you staring towards the shore.'

Ann smoothed her dress. 'What sort of look do you want me to give? Scared? Worried? Excited?'

'Is there any difference, the way you act? Just the look you always give.'

Ann glared at Deadman, then turned and stared pointedly at the shore. Deadman turned the camera.

Moments later the boat grounded on the white sand of the beach and came to rest with a jerk. Ann disappeared over the prow with a screech and a splash.

As his leading lady scrambled to her feet and wrung out the hem of her dress, mouthing imprecations that made the hardened sailors of the boat crew blush and cover their ears, Deadman surveyed the welcoming committee. The islanders seemed to be of all races. Their dress was an *ad hoc* collection of garments reduced to near-rags by time, weather and rough living. Some went bare-chested, others wore loose-fitting shirts, with waistcoats or jerkins over the top. All were barefoot, and most lacked a full complement of eyes, ears or limbs. They were armed with wicked-looking dirks and cutlasses.

A beaming islander wearing ragged, calf-length britches, a leather jerkin and a button reading, 'Hi! I'm Dread Pirate Norman!' stepped forward. 'Oo arrr! Welcome to Dongland!' He made a spacious gesture. 'Our practically finished hotels, almost fully operational fast-food outlets and soon-to-be-completed attractions are very nearly ready and waiting for your pleasure and amusement.'

'Let me handle this.' Indiana vaulted over the side of the boat and advanced up the beach. He gave a gesture of greeting that made the welcoming committee step back and reach for their weapons.

Deadman hurried to his side. 'You seem to be upsetting them, Dr Bones. Leave the talking to me.'

'Please, Deadman.' Indiana gave the movie man a hard stare. 'This is my area of expertise. These people are primitives, easily confused by interaction with a more advanced culture. They appear to speak a dialect of the Mungitungi Islanders.'

'They're speaking perfect English!'

'Yes, but with a very heavy accent. My highly attuned ear can make out some of their meaning.' As Deadman cast his eyes to heaven, Indiana turned to Dread Pirate Norman. 'We come from country far in great iron whale ...'

'Sorry?'

Indiana pointed at the *Vulture* and repeated, in loud and emphatic tones, 'Great iron whale!'

'You mean that rusty old freighter? Sooner you than me.'

Ignoring this, Indiana reached into the boat and brought out a chest. He opened the lid to reveal a collection of gimcrack knives, poorly silvered mirrors and shoddy costume jewellery. 'We bring gifts of great worth.'

Dread Pirate Norman lifted a rope of fake pearls on the point of his dagger. He gave a grimace of distaste. 'Oh, perleeease. Are these Cartier? I don't *think* so.' The rest of the welcoming committee muttered angrily.

'Look, Dr Bones, these people clearly aren't native to this island.' Deadman elbowed Indiana aside. 'Are you?' he demanded.

'Good heavens, no.' Dread Pirate Norman was taken aback. 'We be pirates, ah harrr!'

'Oo-aaaaarrrr,' confirmed the rest of the reception committee.

Deadman nodded. 'Look, friend, we came here to make a movie.'

'You mean you didn't come here to enjoy the forthcoming-any-day-now delights of Dongland, our internationally acclaimed tourist attraction?' Deadman shook his head. Dread Pirate Norman's face fell. 'No, I didn't think so. Can't blame you, really.' He gave the decaying 'attraction' a jaundiced look. 'Rubbish, isn't it?'

Deadman stared at a moth-eaten carousel. Instead of friendly horses and chickens, the ride had a variety of toothy dinosaurs. The producer shuddered. 'Whatever possessed you to build a theme park on a remote island hidden from the rest of the world anyway?'

'Well, after we got stranded here we had to find something to do besides pirating. It seemed like a good idea at the time. We thought we could attract visitors. Some years ago we sent fourteen of the lads off on one of the inflatable dinosaurs from the Jungle Rapids ride to try and drum up some custom, but they never came back.'

'We thought they were refugees from Dong!'

Dread Pirate Norman shook his head. 'Sales reps. But it was a waste of time. We've never had even a single visitor.

Not one. We might as well have built the place in …' His brow furrowed as he tried to think of the most unlikely location imaginable. 'Oh, I dunno. Paris or somewhere.'

'Well, we didn't come here to see Dongland,' said Deadman firmly. 'We're looking for Dong himself.'

Dread Pirate Norman turned pale. 'In that case you'd better come and meet the chief.'

Without another word, he and the reception committee turned and made their way up the beach. Leaving the disgruntled Ray and habitually resentful Obote in charge of the boats, Deadman and his party followed.

CHAPTER SEVEN

By Hook and by Crook

Dread Pirate Norman gestured towards a doorway. 'In there.'

Indiana gripped Deadman's arm. 'Within that dreadful hut,' he intoned portentously, 'lavishly decorated with bones and grinning skulls, the pathetic remains of the tribe's many victims, lurks the leader of these fearsome savages.' He stared the exasperated movie producer straight in the eyes. 'Are you ready to meet the sort of bestial semi-human monster who holds such murderous creatures in thrall?'

' 'Ow do, lads.'

The owner of the voice stepped forward, puffing on a foul banana-leaf cigar and scratching his raggedy backside with the hook on the end of his left arm. He was a balding, pot-bellied old sea-dog with a face like a badly steamed suet pudding and stubble you could strike a match on. He wore khaki shorts, a stained string vest and a barely recognizable tricorn hat with a threadbare skull and crossbones embroidered across the brim.

This apparition greeted his visitors with a cheerful grin. 'Captain 'Oratio Crook, at yer service.'

Ann gave their host a disdainful look. 'Charmed, I'm sure.'

The Captain gave her an appraising glance. 'By gum, bucko' mates 'ave got a lot prettier since I was marooned 'ere.'

'I'll have you know I'm an artiste.' Ann spat accurately an inch from Crook's callused left foot. 'So keep your grubby mitts to yourself, buster.'

Captain Crook gave a fruity chuckle. 'No offence, lass.' Ann elevated her nose and made a great show of attending to her mascara.

Indiana found his voice. 'But – you're a white man!' he protested. 'More or less,' honesty compelled him to add.

Captain Crook scratched at a scab. 'Aye, lad. Well spotted.'

Indiana nodded sagely. 'I see it all – the classic tale. A shipwrecked mariner, accepted and worshipped as a god by benighted savages stricken with awe at their first sight of civilized man.'

Captain Crook rubbed his nose. 'Not quite, lad. For one thing, most of them savages are me crew.'

He paused as something green shot out from behind a hut. Deadman stared as he realized that the newcomer was a boy with a turned-up nose, grinning like a maniac, dressed from head to foot in green, and flying. 'Hiya, Captain Codfish!' the avian urchin called. 'You got some new stiffs to play with?' The boy oriented on Ann and gave a wolf-whistle. 'Who's the broad?'

Ann gave him a withering look. 'Who are you calling a broad, creep?' She gave Deadman a backhanded swipe across the arm. 'Are youse gonna let the little squirt get away with that?'

Deadman shrugged. 'I don't have my rifle. He's probably out of season anyway.'

Captain Crook gave the flying boy a baleful glance. 'You leave me alone, you little devil, I've told you …'

In reply, the boy took his hands from behind his back. They emerged holding a catapult, which the boy used to fire, with startling accuracy, a pebble at the Captain's nose. The pirate howled and lunged at his tormentor. The boy laughed uproariously and shot up to hover just out of reach.

The Captain shook his fist. 'Bugger off, yer little 'ooligan! I'll 'ave an ASBO out on you!'

'Manners, Captain!' The boy stuck his tongue out. 'I'll leave you alone if you'll say you're a codfish.'

'I'll codfish you, you little sod.' The Captain fumbled for his flintlock pistol, but his tormentor was already speeding away across the clearing. The Captain shook his fist at his departing foe and let rip several manly sailor oaths, before turning back to Deadman and Indiana. 'Sorry about that. What were we talking about?'

Indiana was still staring after the retreating figure. 'Who was that?'

Captain Crook gave a sulky shrug. 'Little bugger called Pan. Got it in for me, he has. Kids today, no respect, you try and tell them, you just get a mouthful –'

'You were talking,' Deadman interrupted hastily, 'about how you got to be chief.'

'Aye – but before we get on to that, what are you blokes doing 'ere?' Ann snorted. 'An' lady, o' course. I mean, pleased to meet you and all that, but we don't get many visitors 'ere what with the permanent mysterious mist bank and us bein' five hundred miles from nowhere in particular, an' it's unlikely you were just passin' through the neighbourhood, so I were just wonderin' …'

Indiana and Deadman exchanged glances. Deadman squared his shoulders. 'I'll come straight to the point, Captain. We heard that something lives on this island. Something huge, vile, unspeakable, monstrous.'

'Ah! You've met the wife, then.'

Ann glowered at Captain Crook. 'That was a cheap and obvious gag.'

'Well, it's a cheap and obvious parody.'

Deadman ignored the interruption. 'I'm talking about a creature called Dong – some kind of beast, enormous, terrifying.'

'Aye, 'e's all of that. And that's only part of 'im.'

Deadman could hardly contain his excitement. 'So Dong does exist?'

'Oh, 'e exists all right.'

'Well, my crew and I – and this lovely lady here …' Ann preened. '… have come all the way out here from Hollywood USA to photograph Kong.'

'Is that a fact?' Captain Crook gave a meditative fart. 'You'd better come with me, then. There's some things you should know.'

Indiana gazed in awe at the vast stone wall that cut off the peninsula from the rest of the island. 'Breathtaking! Incredible! To think that such a magnificent structure should be at the mercy of a bunch of primitive savages.'

Ann looked over her shoulder to some of the pirates, who were watching her with undisguised libidinous interest. 'Savages is right.'

Captain Crook was nettled. 'Steady on there, lad.'

The Captain had insisted on taking his visitors on a tour of the island – or to be more accurate, that small part of the island on the seaward side of the wall. Since this mostly consisted of beach pockmarked with unprepossessing real estate in the shape of the pirates' decrepit theme park, tumbledown huts, unhygienic shanties and corrals for a few mangy goats and scrawny chickens, the tour hadn't taken long. But now they had reached the wall, which was a different proposition entirely.

It stood at least fifty feet high, and was constructed of mighty stone blocks that must have weighed many tons apiece. Every inch was covered in off-colour graffiti, bearing messages like *PYRATES ROOL, TIGA LILLY IS A SLAG, LOST BOYZ IN DA HOOD, PEGLEG PETE ♥ BIG FAT NEVILLE, RED INDIANS DO IT IN TEEPEES* and *THE CAPTIN IS A BASTID*.

In the centre of the wall rose enormous gates that seemed to be constructed from the trunks of whole trees. They were held closed by more locks, bolts and chains than would be found on the door of even the most paranoid New York apartment dweller. Above them, and in the walls to either side, was a network of arrow-slots, embrasures and murder holes. The top of the wall was easily wide enough for four men to walk abreast. Above the gate hung an enormous bell.

'As I was saying,' continued Indiana, staring upwards in awe, 'it's a dreadful thought that such a fantastic edifice should languish in the hands of uncouth, ignorant savages who can barely understand the simplest details of its construction.'

'Watch your mouth, Dr Bones.' Deadman, mindful of Captain Crook's scowl, frowned at Indiana. 'We can't afford to antagonize these people.'

Indiana drew himself up to his full height. 'Please, Deadman. I am the expert in primitive cultures, you know. Let me examine this artefact.' He took out a lens and proceeded to a minute investigation of the wall, peering myopically at its structure, feeling the texture of the stone, at one point even tasting its uneven surface. Behind his back, Deadman, Ann and Captain Crook exchanged significant glances.

Indiana concluded his investigations and stepped back. 'It is as I thought,' he said complacently. 'This structure is not the work of the primitive race who currently reside on this island.' He held up a hand to forestall Captain Crook's angry retort. 'Clearly it was made by a far older and more sophisticated culture. Its purpose is, of course, entirely ritualistic.' Crook spluttered. 'It was built as a potent symbol of protection by this ancient people, who then, in the way of antediluvian civilizations, passed from history leaving only this magnificent monument to their genius. Their degenerate descendants –'

Captain Crook could no longer contain his ire. ''Oo are you callin' a descendant?'

'– degenerate descendants,' continued Indiana, ignoring the interruption, 'have of course forgotten the original purpose of the wall and doubtless keep it maintained merely as a tribute to their glorious forebears, in awe of their might and majesty.'

'Bollocks!' roared Captain Crook. 'We keep it maintained because there's a sodding great monster on the other side and it keeps the bloody thing away!'

It took several minutes for Deadman to calm the furious Captain and pacify Indiana, who had gone into a sulk because his expertise was not being taken seriously.

Eventually, he managed to persuade the disgruntled Crook to continue their tour of the island.

The Captain led them to a small hill overlooking the beach. 'I tell you, lads – and lass – this island would be a paradise if it weren't for Dong. Look!' The Captain made a broad gesture, which took in an idyllic scene of islanders relaxing in the warm sun drinking ice-cold pina coladas, strolling hand in hand on the bleached sands and lazily fishing in the warm waters.

'A paradise,' repeated Captain Crook. 'All my lads and lasses want from life are the simple, natural pleasures of lying around on the beach, sipping the milk of coconuts fresh from the tree, and indulging in promiscuous and incestuous sexual relationships.' He made a noise that sounded suspiciously like a sniffle. 'It's not much to ask.' Ann regarded the oiled muscles of some of the more powerfully built of the Captain's pirate crew, and her mouth gave a speculative twitch. She hummed a few bars of 'Mad About the Boy', adjusted her lips into a provocative pout, and allowed one of the straps of her flimsy low-cut summer dress to slip down her shoulder.

Oblivious to this, Crook looked back the way they had come, and his face darkened. 'But there's terrible things the other side of that wall. Beasts the world 'as forgot; bloody great newts as big as a Nantucket whaler, spiders the size of a ship's longboat, great flying lizards that'll have your arm off as soon as look at yer, an' ...' The Captain spluttered, struggling for breath. '... an' – a thing wot ticks.'

Deadman was baffled. 'A thing that ticks? What sort of thing?'

'A toothy thing,' muttered Captain Crook, 'what lies just below the surface o' swamps with only its snout and its little evil slitty eyes showin', still as a log an' quiet as a mousie, going tick, tock, tick, tock, just waitin' to POUNCE WITH ITS EVIL JAWS AGAPE AND CARRY SOME POOR UNSUSPECTIN' MATELOT TO A FOUL WATERY DEATH!'

'Are we talking about a croc—?'

'Shhhh!' Captain Crook leapt at Deadman and clapped a malodorous hand over the movie man's mouth to prevent his completing his sentence. 'We don't mention the C word round hereabouts. Got it?'

'Mmmmuffflgmuggg,' agreed Deadman hastily, making a determined attempt to breathe through his ears.

'Aye.' The Captain released his grip. Deadman fell to his knees, simultaneously gasping for breath and retching from his close encounter with Crook's formidable body odour. 'The interior of this island is a nightmarish hell of creatures

86

that would chomp up a regiment by way of a snack,' added Crook, 'and slurp up the Lord Mayor of London and his whole Corporation for dessert. But there's one beast worse than all the rest, king of that whole murderous, bestial crew – and its name is Dong!'

Indiana gave the brooding trees beyond the wall an apprehensive glance. Ann gasped, mainly for effect. A passing pirate ogled her heaving bosom and walked into a tree.

'But what *is* Dong?' Deadman was beside himself with impatience. 'All we have is a faded, primitive drawing of something terrifying, monstrous, thirty foot –'

'Oh, now, that's a gross exaggeration. Can't be more than fifteen foot at the outside.'

Deadman waved away the interruption. 'Thirty foot *tall*.'

'Oh, yer talkin' about his *height*! Yers, thirty foot, that'd be about right.'

Deadman narrowed his eyes. 'What did you think I was talking about?'

Captain Crook flushed. 'Oh, it doesn't matter.'

Deadman folded his arms and glared at Crook. 'Captain, I have a feeling there's something you're not telling us.'

'Frankly lad, there's a whole bloody lot I'm not telling you. It's a bit much to take in all at one go. Come back to the hut an' I'll try to explain.'

CHAPTER EIGHT

Virgin and the Ridiculous

When they were all settled comfortably outside the chief's hut, drinking a potent native beverage in the shade of an enormous umbrella tree, Captain Crook once again took up his tale.

'Lord knows 'ow long me and the lads 'ave been 'ere. We were doin' a spot of privateerin' along o' Singapore way when we got blown out to sea by a sockin' great storm, an' next thing we knew our faithful barky is drivin' onto the reef an' smashin' herself to smithereens, an' we're shipwrecked on this island. There was practically no one 'ere, then, apart from a few native wenches.'

Ann pursed her lips. 'I guess I can imagine what happened to *them*.'

Crook looked pained. 'Well, we *are* pirates, lass. Fair do's. Anyway, we felt we 'ad a duty to repopulate the island. Some of the keener lads were repopulatin' it two or three times a night from what I 'eard. Enjoyin' yer drinks, then?'

Indiana nodded. 'It's good. What is it?'

'Kava.' The Captain took a healthy swig and swilled it around his mouth appreciatively. 'We make it by chewin' up the roots of the kava plant and spittin' into a dirty big bucket. Then we leave it to fester in the sun for a week or two. Then we drink it.'

Poker-faced, Deadman put his drink down. Anne poured hers carefully onto the ground beside her, and covered the wet patch with sand. Indiana offered his drink to a mangy pi-dog. The animal looked at it suspiciously, took one lick, gave a startled whimper and promptly expired.

Captain Crook took another swig of the vile fluid. 'I was Captain, of course, so I became chief o' the island. It wasn't until later that I found the job 'ad its ... drawbacks.'

'Such as?'

'Well, for starters, there's the beasties I mentioned earlier. Creatures what became extinct millions of years ago, but still living in the primeval hell up on top o' that unscalable precipice. Any argy-bargy from them, an' it's muggins 'ere 'as to sort it out.'

Deadman nodded wisely. 'So you built the wall?'

'Not us, lad. Like Mister Primitive Savages there said ...' (Indiana glowered at the jibe.) '... that were there already. Built by some 'ighly advanced race what'd died off before we got 'ere.'

'What happened to them?'

'I dunno.' Captain Crook gazed balefully at the wall and the precipitous cliffs beyond. 'But I can guess. Any'ow, when we first got 'ere we set out to explore the hinterior.' The Captain shuddered. ''Orrible place it is. We lost six o' the lads in the first 'alf mile – stomped, chewed, poisoned or just disappeared without a trace. Fearless Fred ran off yellin' for 'is mum, Desperate Dave was, and Invincible Ivan turned out not to be. Anyway, after that we stayed this side o' the gate an' doubled the locks. We set up Dongland to make some sort o' ready cash, but to be 'onest the whole malarkey was a bit of a fiasco. But we ain't about to go the other side of that wall again, not for nothing. All them bloodthirsty beasts, not to mention flyin' kids.'

'Like that Pan person?'

'Aye, and there's others – the Lost Boys they call themselves, little 'ooligans I call 'em. I blame the parents – least, I would if they 'ad any. And then there's that Tiger Lilly an' 'er Red Indians an' – that thing as ticks.'

'You mean, the croc— mmmmffff.'

'Like I said before, we don't mention the C word, if it's all the same to you. All right?'

'Sure thing,' said Deadman in a muffled voice. 'Could you please stop sitting on my head now?'

Scowling, the Captain released the suffocating producer. ''Ark to my advice, lads. Don't set foot the other side of that wall. All yer'll find is rottin' vegetation, stagnant swamps an' graspin' bloodthirsty leeches.'

'Sounds just like parts of Queens,' murmured Ann.

'Take my word for it. There's nothin' for yer out there but misery, sudden death and ...' The old pirate shuddered. 'Dong.'

'That's what we've come here to find!' exclaimed Deadman. 'But you still haven't told us what it is!'

Captain Crook gave the movie-maker a sideways look. ''Appen you'll find out for yourself if you stick around 'ere for a bit. 'E's the strongest beast on the island. Boss o' the whole show.' He jerked a grimy thumb at the mountain that dominated the interior. 'Lives up there wi' his mate, Marzipan.'

'Marzipan!' Indiana let out a low whistle. 'So the legends are true!'

'What legends?' said Deadman.

'The primitive tribes of this region tell tales of Marzipan, Lord of the Jungle,' said Indiana. 'He's a white man, abandoned in the forest in infancy and raised by a family of apes. The legend says he wears nothing but a loincloth fashioned from the pelt of a leopard he killed himself with his bare hands; and that he has uncanny strength and agility, and the power to communicate with animals who recognize him as their master.'

Ann raised her hand. 'Did you say "loincloth"?'

'Apparently, having lived all those years with apes,' Indiana concluded, 'he learnt their way of life.'

'Are we talking about one of those brief, revealing loincloths?' Ann's eyes went misty as her imagination got to work.

'Learnt too bloody much about their way of life, if you ask me.' The Captain looked around cagily and lowered his voice. 'I speak as I find, lads. I'm not one to judge, but to my mind, Marzipan livin' up there in that cave with old Dong – well, it's not natural.'

'Not natural?' Deadman boggled. 'A human being brought up by apes and running round in a furry posing-pouch talking to animals? Of course it's not goddamn natural!'

'No, I mean …' The Captain shrugged. 'Well, you'll find out. 'E's all right, Marzipan – comes down to the village reg'lar for supplies. But Dong – well, 'e's been top dog round 'ere for so long, 'e won't take no for an answer. Them old people as built this wall, they used to do human sacrifices to keep 'im quiet – so when we turn up there's nothin' for it but *we* 'ave to do human sacrifices for 'im as well. Or else. An' the lads decided, democratically like, that as I was the chief it was up ter me ter sacrifice my wife ter Dong.'

'Your wife?' Indiana was scandalized.

Ann looked daggers at Crook. 'It's always the goil who suffers.'

'According to the stories I heard,' said Deadman carefully, 'it was only virgins got sacrificed to Dong.'

'Well, technic'ly, yes,' said Captain Crook, looking shifty. 'But I reckon them old people died off 'cos they ran out of virgins, and us bein' pirates, we didn't 'ave many around to start off with – apart from Spotty Ken, and even Dong'd draw the line at '*im*. We reckoned the rules'd have to be interpreted flexibly, like. So we worked out we'd let 'im 'ave women who had, at some point, *been* virgins, and everyone was 'appy.'

'Just a minute!' Indiana pointed an accusing finger at Captain Crook. 'Did you or did you not just tell us you sacrificed your wife to Dong?'

'Oh, aye,' said Captain Crook placidly. 'Well, I didn't

93

'ave no choice in the matter, what with me bein' chief an' all.' He raised his voice and called over his shoulder. 'Ey, Wendy! I'm tellin' these lads 'ow I sacrificed yer ter Dong.'

A matronly woman in bleached hair and a sarong emerged from the hut. 'Aye,' she said, 'he did an' all.'

'Wendy?' Indiana stared from Wendy to her husband and back again. 'Not "Wendy" as in "Darling"?'

The woman nodded.

Ann gave her a contemptuous look. 'No relation,' she said decisively.

But Indiana was still gawping at Wendy. 'Do you mean to say –'

'Aye, lad.' Captain Crook gave him a knowing leer. 'She come 'ere with that little bugger Pan, but she grew up an' 'e never did. Work it out for yerself.'

Wendy nodded. 'Aye. I thought that Peter were the cat's pyjamas when I were little – but then I started gettin' interested in … you know, *feelins* – kissin' an' cuddlin' an that – and all he were interested in was havin' farting competitions an' seein' who could pee furthest up the wall. Well, I like a laugh as much as the next person, but a woman 'as *needs*.'

The Captain nodded smugly. 'So next time I kidnapped 'er, and that little flyin' sod came to rescue 'er, she told 'im to bugger off, an' we've been together ever since.' He gave Wendy's ample rump a lascivious squeeze.

'Get off, yer big soft devil.' Wendy batted his hand away in mock outrage. Crook gave a fruity chuckle.

'What a story!' Deadman rubbed his hands gleefully. 'This is going to make my fortune. It's the blockbuster to end all blockbusters, the greatest story ever told. It's got everything! Pirates! An ape-man! A terrifying monster! A struggling, weeping, helpless maiden, offered to the rampaging beast as a virgin sacrifice …'

Ann gave him a jaundiced look. 'Would that be me, by any chance?'

'Well, er …'

Ann folded her arms and drew herself up. 'And what happens to these poor helpless victims, if I may be so bold as to enquire?'

'According to legend,' said Indiana, oblivious to Deadman's frantic shushing motions, 'Dong's sacrificial victims are hideously mutilated in the monster's vile attempts to satisfy its depraved sexual appetites before being torn limb from limb, ending up as an unrecognizably mangled corpse.'

'Peachy!' Ann gave Deadman a killing look.

'Oh, no, love.' Wendy gave Ann a pat on the arm.

'Generally he carries me back to 'is cave, an' I do a bit of sweepin' an' dustin' before he forgets I'm there and then I sneak home. How many times have you sacrificed me to Dong, 'Orrie?'

Captain Crook's lips moved as he counted his fingers. 'Let's see – counting leap years but not the time you 'ad lumbago and we 'ad to sacrifice me in a blonde wig instead – thirty-seven.'

'Thirty-eight. You're forgettin' bank holidays.'

'Oh, aye.' Crook beamed at his visitors. 'I think virgin sacrifices are pretty much force of 'abit with 'im, to be truthful. 'E don't really seem interested. If you ask me, 'e's only got eyes for Marzipan.'

'Now, 'usband,' chided Wendy, 'you mustn't be spreadin' gossip.'

'Well, lass, I speak as I find, an' if the cap fits … All I'm sayin' is, if Dong 'as a virgin sacrifice at 'is beck an' call, an' she finds 'erself doin' a bit o' light dustin' while 'e's swingin' from tree to tree after some beefcake wi' ripplin' muscles in a pair o' leopard-skin Y fronts – well, not to beat about the bush, when it comes to Dong and Marzipan, it's not 'ard to see which side their bread's buttered.'

Deadman looked like a kid who had just found out the candy store had closed. 'Sweeping? Dusting? That doesn't sound like it's gonna set the audience squirming with terror. Still, maybe we can pep it up a little.' The movie mogul was suddenly silenced as, from far away on the other side of the wall, there echoed a savage, blood-curdling cry …

'Aaah-*aaa*-ahhh-*aaa*-ahhh, *aaa*-ahhh-*aaa*-ahhh!'

Deadman turned pale. 'My god! What was that?'

Ann clutched at Wendy's arm. 'Was it a bird?'

Indiana scanned the skies. 'Was it a plane?'

Captain Crook shook his head. 'That was 'im,' he said in hushed tones. 'Marzipan, Lord of the Jungle.'

'The Lord of the Jungle.' Deadman's voice was reverential. 'Is he issuing a challenge? Reinforcing his claim to his territory? Summoning his faithful animal companions to his side?'

Captain Crook flushed. 'No. That's – 'ow can I put this delicately? – that's the noise you make during sexual congress when your lover is a thirty-foot gorilla.'

CHAPTER NINE

A Taste of Marzipan

There was a brief shocked silence as the visitors absorbed what they had just heard.

'You're saying that this Marzipan has a ... "relationship" ... with a thirty-foot ape?' gasped Deadman.

'Give or take a couple of inches,' nodded the Captain.

Ann arched an eyebrow. 'By the sound that boy was making, he was taking more than a couple of inches!'

Indiana's mouth hung open like an excavator bucket. 'A physical relationship?'

Captain Crook shrugged. 'I said it weren't natural.'

Deadman shook his head. 'That is sick! It's terrible! Appalling! Degrading!' His face lit up. 'What a movie it's gonna make! This is getting better and better!'

'Datin' gorillas? Nothin' new there,' muttered Ann. 'I've been doin' it for years.'

Indiana gave her a shocked stare. 'If you knew they were the type to make … advances, why did you date them?'

Ann's lip curled. 'What's your problem, Mr Squeaky Clean? I bet you've dated a few flappers in your time.'

'Actually, no,' said Indiana haughtily. 'If you must know, I'm saving myself for the right person.'

'No kiddin'? Hey, Captain!' said Ann. 'Sounds like you just found yourselves a real virgin sacrifice for this Dong.'

'I don't see why you feel the need to make fun of me,' whined Indiana, 'just because I choose to keep myself pure.'

'That's an easy choice to make,' drawled Ann, 'when no goil would touch you with a thirty-foot pole.'

Indiana stormed out of the hut with the others' mocking laughter ringing in his ears.

The Captain took another gulp of Kava and smacked his lips. 'Well, mateys, I reckons we've been friggin' in the riggin' for long enough. It's time we got down to business.'

'Business?' said Deadman suspiciously. 'What business? Like I told you, we're here to shoot a movie.'

'Exactly. There's no business like show business.' The Captain smiled, revealing a row of blackened teeth. 'I don't know 'ow you're goin' ter do this movie thing of yours without some 'elp.'

'Help? What sort of help?' said Deadman slowly and suspiciously.

''*Elp*, 'elp.' The Captain leaned forward, his hook glinting in the sunlight. 'I mean ter say, 'ow could you get this movie of yours filmed if the natives became a bit unfriendly like, or if some o' your equipment suddenly disappeared or even unexpectedly and inexplicably caught fire? You'd need 'elp makin' sure that sort 'f thing don't 'appen.' The Captain gave Deadman a leering wink. 'As it 'appens, and luckily for you, as the chief of Skulland-crossbones Island and CEO of Dongland, I'm in a position to provide that 'elp in exchange for certain sums of money.'

'You're blackmailing me,' said Deadman impassively.

'I'm a pirate,' said Crook. 'Old 'abits die hard. Dongland isn't the chest of gold I thought it'd be and the bottom's fallen out o' the pensions market, I need to think of me and my Wendy's future. Unlike that little bugger Pan and his ruddy Lost Boys, some of us are getting older. And blackmail is an ugly word. I'd prefer to consider this as insurance.'

'Blackmail is usually a damn sight cheaper than insurance,' said Deadman grimly. 'OK, OK, I get your drift.' He reached into his pocket. 'How about a hundred bucks?'

The Captain considered momentarily. 'Or,' he said, ''ow about location shooting fees to include a negotiating fee for myself and my associates ...' (The Captain winked at Wendy.) '... regarding the rental o' jungle sets and supplying of extras on a daily pro rata basis plus fifty per cent of total cost of said provision in addition to a contract for the exclusive supply of all catering and accommodation plus a straight twenty per cent of box office return (worldwide), a negotiated percentage for any digital exploitation in all present and known forms, exclusive rights for all actors' interviews with magazines and newspapers, and twenty-five per cent of all commercial marketing exploitation rights.' The Captain paused to take a breath. 'All figures based on gross income, of course,' he added.

There was a silence as Deadman eyed up the Captain. 'For an old sea captain stranded on a god-forsaken island in the middle of nowhere, you seem to know a lot about the movie business.'

'A pirate is a pirate, lad, whether he's marooned on a desert island or eating executive lunches in 'Ollywood.'

'Come on, Deadman,' said Ann. 'Give the guy what he wants so we can shoot the movie and get off this island sooner rather than later. This sun and salt are playing havoc with my hair.'

'Yeah, turning it back to its natural colour,' muttered Deadman. He turned to the Captain. 'OK, Crook, you got me over a barrel. But I gotta proposition for you. Instead of paying up front, I'll make you an executive producer. It's a better deal. You get fifty per cent of all profits and your name up in lights! Just imagine, "Deadman and Crook Pictures present".'

'C before D,' said Wendy.

'What?'

'Crook comes before Deadman.'

The producer shook his head. 'OK, OK. Jeez, you want the shirt off my back as well? "Crook and Deadman" it is.'

Brow furrowed, the Captain scratched at his nose with his hook as he considered. 'OK, we got a deal. Shake on it.'

'*Ow!*' screamed Deadman.

The Captain pulled back his hook. 'Sorry about that. I sometimes get my 'ook and my 'and mixed up when I'm excited.'

'Good job you're married and don't spend time on your own, then.' Deadman pulled out a handkerchief and wrapped it round his bleeding fist as Crook and Wendy leapt up and toasted each other with Kava, before breaking into a celebration dance and screams of 'We're rich!'

Ann sidled up to Deadman. 'I thought you were supposed to be a big-shot producer? You've just given half the film away.'

Ignoring his aching wound, Deadman gave Ann a wink. 'He's an executive producer. He might as well be the Man in the Moon! It's a classic Hollywood scam to get something for nothing – give the schmuck a title and the promise of money in the future and he'll agree to anything. It's all stardust – glitter and glamour. Don't worry; he'll never see a nickel. Even when it's a blockbusting success, once my accountants have got hold of the books this film will have made such a loss he'll be paying me! He don't know it yet, but he's the one over a barrel!'

Before Ann could reply, the air was once again rent with an unholy cry.

'Aaah-*aaa*-ahhh-*aaa*-ahhh, *aaa*-ahhh-*aaa*-ahhh!'

Deadman looked up. 'Sounds like someone else is over a barrel.'

Ann took a deep breath. '*Twice* within half an hour? That Dong must be one hell of a beast!'

103

Next day the pirates' village was alive with preparations for filming. Supplies and photographic equipment had been shipped off the *Vulture* by the rag-bag crew and the ever-protesting Obote. 'Will you feel the weight of this thing? Is this within the limits set by the Manual Handling Operations Regulations as defined by the Health and Safety at Work Executive? I don't *think* so! Did you know that thirty-eight per cent of all work-related injuries are musculoskeletal disorders brought about by excessive loads and inappropriate lifting techniques?'

WHACK!

The bosun grinned. 'And a further ten per cent are caused by know-all loafers being smacked on the head with my belaying pin,' he told the unconscious Obote. 'Now, the rest of you men – get moving!'

The work continued apace. Among the crates unloaded were several with stencilled warnings:

KEEP OUT!
TOP SECRET!
NOT CONTRABRAND – HONEST

These were now stacked on the beach, and under Deadman's orders armed guards ensured no one could get near them. Indiana's enquiries into what was in the boxes received short shrift from Deadman, who told him to keep his goddamn nose out of things that didn't concern him.

Crook had been true to his word, if not his name, and mustered his men to appear as extras. These now milled around the *Vulture*'s crew trying to sell them Dongburgers, Donga-Cola, banana-flavoured candyfloss and a variety of tacky souvenirs including Lucky Dong key rings, Dong glow-in-the-dark pencil sharpeners, and Dong T-shirts, mugs, coasters and fridge magnets.

While Deadman organized his armed guards, Ann lounged in a hammock, sipping at a Kava-free cocktail from the ship's stores. A book rested on her thigh as she swung gently in the breeze. She was eyeing up the pirates and making a mental list of 'chores' (as in 'Chore place or mine?') when Indiana appeared at the side of the hammock.

'Hi there,' he began. 'How you doing?'

'Just dandy until you turned up.'

There was a silence while Indiana tried to think of something witty and pithy. He failed. 'The sun's hot.'

'Don't touch it then.'

More silence.

'What are you reading?'

'A book.'

In desperation, Indiana gestured towards the drink. 'What's your pleasure?'

'A slow comfortable screw,' said Ann deliberately. 'And it don't involve you. I'm busy now. Can I ignore you some other time?'

Indiana's face was a picture of misery. 'Ann, don't be that way. I've got ... feelings for you. You're the first girl I've ever met who meant something.' Ignoring Ann's yawn, Indiana continued. 'Do you think you could ever fall for me?'

'Only if you pushed me out of this hammock.'

'But I could be good for you,' pleaded Indiana. 'I'll always be there for you.'

'Why didn't you say so?'

Indiana's eyes lit up. Briefly.

'You can be there and I can be someplace else.'

Indiana looked crestfallen. 'You're making a big mistake here. Guys like me don't grow on trees.'

'No, they usually swing from them.'

Indiana was almost in tears. 'I can look after you.'

Ann stared at Indiana. 'Listen, buster, I'm from Brooklyn. Does it look as though I *need* lookin' after?'

Indian bristled. 'Maybe you do! What about Deadman? He's brought you to this island in the middle of nowhere and now he's got armed guards for all those crates. What's that all about? And what's he got planned for you and Dong? I don't trust him.'

'Since when did anyone trust a Hollywood producer?'

'But I love you!' declared Indiana.

'Oh perlease!'

'I'd die for you.'

'Do you have a schedule for that?' Ann shook her head. 'Why don't you just push off? I'm preparing for my part.' She took another sip of her drink.

'You have no heart!' wailed Indiana. 'And neither do I! You've broken it! I'm leaving. For good!'

'Bye. Don't write.'

With a broken sob, Indiana turned and stormed off along the beach.

'Whatta sap!' muttered Ann. She looked up as a crescendo of noise broke out among the villagers. Shading her eyes from the glare of the sun, she glanced over to see what was the cause of the commotion.

Sweating pirates were hauling at the great gate in the centre of the wall. As it creaked reluctantly open, a figure appeared, striding with a peculiar, bow-legged gait down the jungle path into the village. The newcomer was a bronzed beefcake whose muscles rippled with his every step. Dark hair flicked at his shoulders. He was naked save for a leopard-skin loincloth that barely covered his assets.

Seeing this vision, Ann flipped herself out of the hammock and casually strolled over to meet the Adonis at a speed that would have outstripped an Olympic sprinter. Within the blink of an eye, she had pushed her way through the villagers and was standing next to the hunk offering him her hand ('And anything else he wants,' she thought). She broke into a dazzling smile. 'Hi, I'm Ann Darling and I don't sleep with strangers. So what's your name?'

The loinclothed figure swept back his dark locks. 'Me Marzipan.'

'"Me Marzipan"?' she repeated. 'You got a stutter?'

The newcomer grimaced. 'Marzipan sorry. Marzipan not used to intercourse with humans.'

Ann's lips pursed. 'Killjoy.'

'Marzipan mean intercourse in sense of verbal communication,' said the new arrival hastily, 'not in sense of –'

'Hi there!' Deadman had heard the commotion caused by Marzipan's appearance and made his way from the beach. He pushed his way through the throng surrounding the loinclothed figure. 'Who we got here?'

'Me Marzipan. Damn! Marzipan apologize. Marzipan find pronouns difficult, not to mention verb agreements.'

A Taste of Marzipan

Deadman raised an eyebrow. 'Is this guy for real?'

Ann sighed. 'Yes, oh yes!'

'Marzipan take time to assimilate with humans. Marzipan and Dong speak in ape language: all grunting and groaning.'

'We heard,' said Ann. 'Several times.'

Curious as to the identity of the new arrival, Ray simpered over. Taking in the vision before him, his eyes widened. 'And who is this chunk of loveliness? I don't believe I've had the pleasure ... yet.'

Ann stepped forward and took Marzipan by the arm. 'Back off, you little mince,' she warned. 'First law of salvage – first to hook it, gets it. My claws are already in.'

Ray bridled. 'And you're the expert on hooking.'

'Cool it, girls,' ordered Deadman. 'Ray, this is the guy Crook told us about last night – Marzipan, the legendary Lord of the Jungle.'

'How sweet!' Ray's eyes glinted. Saliva appeared at the sides of his mouth. 'I love marzipan! But with this voyage and whatnot, it's been a long time since I've had my tongue round a bit of marzipan.'

Deadman groaned. 'Ray, that wasn't even a single entendre. For the sake of common decency, any chance of keeping them double?'

But Ray was in full flow as he bathed in the sight of muscled manhood standing before him. 'The loincloth I like. It's so …' he licked his lips, '… primitive, yet so *now*. Revealing, but intriguing – the promise of hidden delights and earthly pleasures …'

'If you froth at the mouth any more,' snapped Ann, 'we're gonna have to give you a rabies shot.'

Ray's eyes narrowed and his lips pouted. 'There's only one dog around here.' He turned back to Marzipan, running his hands down the huge muscled forearm. 'Oh yes. The loincloth, I like. But I know what would look better on you …' Ray gave an outrageous wink. 'Me!'

Deadman's eyes rose heavenwards. 'Ray, stop acting the fool.'

'Who's acting?' spat Ann.

'So, Marzipan,' interrupted Deadman in an effort to stop the brewing cat-fight, 'how did you get here?'

'Marzipan son of Lord and Lady Grey of Castle Greyskull, owners of Greyfriars School and trainers of Greyfriars Bobby, well-known necrophiliac dog. Marzipan's parents explorers, seeking Lost City of Shangri-la.'

'But Shangri-la is supposed to be in Asia,' protested Deadman. 'How come they ended up on this island?'

'Marzipan not say they were *good* explorers. Marzipan

abandoned in jungle when mother and father eaten by giant prehistoric tadpoles. Marzipan not die, Marzipan rescued by apes. Marzipan and Dong become friends. Marzipan realize that relationship develop beyond normal man–ape friendship. Marzipan move into Dong's cave as equal partner in mutually fulfilling and beneficial same-sex relationship.'

'Well, that story was succinct and to the point despite being full of anomalies such as not explaining how a man raised by apes can speak nearly perfect English,' said Deadman.

Marzipan shook his head unhappily. 'Marzipan not good at English. Marzipan frequently confuse nominative and accusative. Marzipan crap with apostrophes. Marzipan not recognize subjunctive mode if it fell on him.'

Ray shuddered. 'You poor dear. It must be just awful for you – living in a cold dank cave with an insatiable, savage monster taking carnal pleasures from you at his every whim.'

'It could have been worse,' said Obote. 'He could have gone to an English public school.'

'How the hell do you know what happens at an English public school?' demanded Deadman.

'Just because I'm black you got no right to assume that I didn't experience an English education.'

'And did you?'

'No – but only because my parents refused to have

anything to do with a socially divisive school system based on outmoded concepts of class and privilege.'

As Deadman racked his brains for a cutting reply, Captain Crook arrived on the scene. 'Ah, I see you've met Marzipan. Mornin', Marzie. 'Ow's tricks on the other side o' the wall?'

'Marzipan tickety-boo and ding-dong.'

'I bet,' said Ann, her eyes still riveted to Marzipan's inadequate furry posing-pouch.

'We 'aven't 'ad the pleasure of yer company for some time,' remarked Crook. 'What brings yer down 'ere, Marzie-boy?'

Marzipan looked embarrassed. 'Marzipan need medication for Marzipan's ... Marzipan's ...' His voice fell to a whisper. 'You know.'

'Yer piles playin' up again, are they?' roared the Captain. Marzipan turned a deep shade of red. 'I'm not surprised with that bloody great ape doin' what 'e does!' Crook winked at the others. 'Round 'ere, we call this lad "Marzipan of the Grapes" on account of 'is great hanging ...'

'Thank you, Captain,' cut in Deadman, clenching his buttocks as tightly as he could. 'Too much information.'

The Captain held up his hook. 'I could always operate.'

He left the suggestion hanging in the air. Marzipan turned from red to green, changing colour like a traffic light. Crook shrugged. 'Suit yourself. One o' you lads go catch a shark and get Mrs Crook to make up some of 'er arse liniment for the lad.'

As one of the pirates scuttled away to do the Captain's bidding, Deadman gave the Lord of the Jungle a comradely slap on the back. 'Hey, Marzipan, you're Dong's best buddy – maybe you could help us out here.' He began explaining about the movie.

Ann was standing with her eyes closed and her mouth working. After a moment or two she sidled up to Crook. 'OK, I'll buy it. Why d'you need a shark?'

'Shark oil's good fer piles.' The Captain winked at Ann. 'A few drops and 'is grapes'll be raisins.'

'Shark oil?' Ann looked bemused. 'How ever did you find out that shark oil cures piles?'

Crook gave an involuntary shudder. 'By trial and very painful error.'

'So maybe with your help,' Deadman concluded, 'we could get Dong to cooperate with the filming of the virgin sacrifice.'

The Lord of the Jungle shook his head. 'Marzipan think that could be a problem.'

Deadman breathed a big sigh. 'OK, OK, I understand. You can be an executive producer.'

'Marzipan not angling for name on credits. Marzipan and Dong have tiff. Marzipan feel sore and Dong want to play "hide the banana". Marzipan say, "No more" and Dong throw wobbler. Marzipan argue with Dong and inadvertently give game away.'

The Captain's eyes widened. 'What's yer meanin', lad?'

Marzipan looked uncomfortable, as well he might. 'Marzipan lose rag and go off on one. Marzipan tell Dong he stupid ape with brains of retarded baboon. Marzipan ask Dong if he so clever why he fooled by pirates for years by them offering same virgin for sacrifice?'

''Ell and tarnation,' howled Crook. 'You've got a mouth as big as his.'

'Marzipan know. Marzipan sorry.' Marzipan spread his hands in helpless apology. 'Marzipan come to warn Crook. Dong doing his nut. Dong mad as a cut snake. If Dong not given proper top-hole virgin next time, Dong smash down wall and destroy village.'

CHAPTER TEN

Monkey Business

'Well, Captain Crook,' drawled Deadman, 'it sounds like you and your pirates have a problem.'

Crook gave the movie man a hard stare. 'No, Mr Deadman. We've *both* got a problem. I may be chief o' this 'ere island, but I can't very well supply you with extras on a daily pro rata basis and provide for all yer catering and accommodation needs if Dong goes apeshit, kicks seven barrels out o' my lads, and wrecks the whole bloody village, now can I? Not to mention as I don't suppose for an instant, if he comes rampagin' down 'ere, 'e's going to stop to ask 'isself whether 'e's bashin' up my lads and property, or yours. You follow me?'

Deadman looked thoughtful.

'No, lad.' Crook's tone was grim. 'There's only one way out of this 'ere predicament. We need ter find a virgin.'

Deadman laughed. 'Lots of luck!'

'And it can't be one of our lasses,' continued Crook as though Deadman had not spoken, 'because a) we 'aven't got no virgins, and b) even if we 'ad, the lads'd never wear it. The chief 'as to provide the sacrifice, see, and now Dong 'as twigged about our Wendy, I'm fresh out of virgins; even, so to speak, retired ones.'

Deadman eyed the old pirate narrowly. 'Mind if I have a word in private with you, Captain?' Then, without turning his head, he said, 'Ann, honey, why don't you go off and powder your nose.'

'If you mean take a leak, I don't need –'

'I'm trying politely to invite you to take your butt out of here while I have a private conference with the Captain. Go on, beat it.'

'That ain't no way to treat a lady!'

'Yeah? Well, if I meet one I'll try to put in some practice. Scram.'

Ann flounced off, almost colliding with the pirate who had come to announce that Marzipan's pile ointment was ready. Marzipan followed the man in a chimpanzee crouch.

Crook and Deadman made their way to the pirate captain's hut. When the door was closed, Deadman turned to Crook. 'What's on your mind?'

'Well, we're men of the world, you and me, right, Mr Deadman?' Deadman said nothing. Crook sighed. 'All right then, cards on the table. Yer crew 'aven't seen a woman in weeks, 'cept for Miss Darling – and she can't satisfy the needs of all o' them.'

'Oh, believe me, she's tried.'

'Well, I'm willin' to offer you six lasses of ours, all o' them practically virgins.' Deadman raised an eyebrow. 'All right, let's just say comparatively young women of marriageable age, who'll keep those lusty lads o' yours 'appy all the way back home. And in return, all I'm askin' as that you let us sacrifice your Miss Darling ter Dong. Wench like that, bit o' class, just what we need ter keep the old bugger 'appy.'

'Are you crazy?' cried Deadman. 'You can't expect me to be an accomplice to such a sickening, barbaric act of savagery!'

'Bloody 'ell, lad, it's nothing of the kind. If we don't find old Dong a top-notch virgin our lives won't be worth livin'. We need a Beauty to satisfy the Beast – and to be honest, the women round 'ere don't qualify. It's the sea air and constant drudgery – ages 'em faster than workin' fer a contract cleaning company.'

'But *Ann* …' Deadman shook his head. 'You can't be serious!'

Crook sniffed. 'I s'pose you find the suggestion offensive.'

'No, just impractical. For one thing, I have good reason to believe that Ann Darling hasn't been a virgin since Prohibition started – wouldn't that disqualify her?'

Crook gave him a knowing grin. 'Come on, lad, he's a sodding monkey. How's he going to know the difference?'

Deadman said nothing. He sat without moving, his lips pursed in thought.

The crafty old pirate leaned forward. In confidential tones, he said, 'And just think. A virgin sacrifice ter Dong! What a scene that would make for this movie o' yours.'

'Say, you're right.' Deadman nodded slowly. 'Maybe we *can* cut a deal …'

'All right, loves!' Ray hauled the lid off the final crate. 'Line up for your cossies, and no pushing!'

The pirates stepped forward cautiously. They peered into the crates. They looked at each other.

One drew his cutlass and poked it into the crate.

He withdrew it with a frilly shirt dangling from the point. 'What be this, matey?'

Ray snatched the costume. 'Watch what you're doing with that nasty great sword, you'll snag the material!' He held the shirt across his chest and said, as though explaining to a very small child, 'It's a *pirate* costume, sweetheart. You have to get dressed up as *pirates*.'

The man who had taken out the shirt looked bewildered. 'We *are* dressed as pirates.'

'No you're not! Pirates don't dress like that!'

'But we *are* pirates! This is what we wear.'

'No it *isn't*.' Ray raised his eyes to the heavens. Then he stepped forward and put an arm round the pirate's shoulder. 'Look, babes. This is the movies, *capisce*? The audience has expectations. When they think "pirates", they think Douggie Fairbanks Jr, you get me?' He gave the ragged pirates a disdainful stare. 'They don't think a bunch of refugees from a soup kitchen.' He held out the shirt and shook it. 'This is what the punters think pirates wear, so if you're gonna be in Mr Deadman's movie, this is what you wear, OK?'

Muttering, the pirates rummaged through the costumes, giving pained exclamations at their finds.

'Look at this shirt! Floppy sleeves – and a gathered waist …'

'This waistcoat is *embroidered*.'

'There's a damn great ribbon here.'

'It's a sash!' hissed Ray. 'It goes round your waist.'

'Not round *my* waist, it doesn't!'

'I can't wear this headscarf!'

'Why not?' grated Ray.

'Well, I ask you, just look at it.'

'It's a very nice colour,' Ray insisted.

'Sod the colour! It's got lace round the edge. And *beads*.'

Deadman strode on to the scene wearing regulation director's jodhpurs and carrying a megaphone. 'What's going on here, Ray?'

'I'm sorry, Mr Deadman.' Ray's manner was veering towards the hysterical. 'The pirates don't want to look like pirates.'

'But I don't want pirates!' Deadman told him.

Ray clapped a hand to his cheek. 'You don't want pirates?'

'Hell, no. What would pirates be doing on a desert island?'

'But there *are* pirates on this –'

'Ray.' Deadman gave the quivering designer an avuncular smile. 'This is a jungle movie, right? Giant apes. Primeval forests. Deadly creepy-crawlies. And dusky savages. Witch doctors. Mumbo jumbo. Cannibalistic rituals. Voodoo.

120

Wild native dances and human sacrifice. See? We put pirates in this movie, we're mixing our genres, we're gonna confuse the audience. God knows it doesn't take much. Now, take back the pirate costumes, OK? And I want every extra on this set wearing a grass skirt, a bone necklace and a tin of boot polish half an hour from now. Got it?'

'Yes, Mr Deadman,' moaned Ray. He staggered off to put Deadman's orders into effect.

'Dusky savages, eh?'

Deadman turned. Able Seaman Obote was leaning against the trunk of a palm tree with a satirical glint in his eye. Deadman glared at him. 'Is there some comment you wish to make?'

'No, sir.' Obote returned Deadman's glare with an insolent grin. 'I wasn't going to say a thing.'

'Good.' Deadman watched poker-faced as Ray bullied and cajoled the resentful extras into swapping their pirate costumes for Hollywood's idea of native dress, and blacking up. This was what location shooting was all about: endless arguments and delays followed by a few seconds' filming during which the only cloud in the sky would cover the sun for the first time all day.

At length, when Captain Crook's reluctant crew had been tinted to Ray's satisfaction, Deadman stepped forward and raised his megaphone. 'OK, people. We've got a big scene to shoot, so I need your full attention and cooperation. Now this is the scene where you prepare the heroine for the sacrifice.' He broke off, scanning the crowd. 'Where is Miss Darling? Ray?' Deadman stifled an oath as the costumier scuttled off to the thatched hut that Ann insisted on referring to as her 'trailer'.

'OK, the rest of you. I want two girls – you and you.' Deadman pointed to two of the pirates' more presentable concubines, who at least had most of their teeth. He continued, 'You're anointing the virgin with garlands of flowers, OK? Preparing her to be the Bride of Dong. Now, the rest of you ...' He pointed to the others. 'I want wild, abandoned native dancing as you work yourselves up into a frenzy for the sacrifice.'

The extras looked at the ground and shuffled their feet.

'Is there a problem?' growled Deadman.

A villainous-looking pirate with a fake bone through his nose said, 'Beg pardon, Mr Deadman, but we're pirates. We don't know nothin' about wild native dancin'.'

'We could do a hornpipe,' contributed a second pirate.

The others nodded agreement. 'Maybe if we had a choreographer ...'

'Jeez!' Deadman clenched his fists and swore. 'What do

you think my name is, Busby Freakin' Berkeley? You just shuffle round in a circle and every few seconds beat your chests, then you throw your hands up in the air and shout "Dong!" How hard can it be?'

''Scuse me, Mr Deadman.' Obote detached himself from the tree and stepped forward. 'I could teach these guys a native dance.'

Deadman stared at him. 'You know about native dancing?'

'Yessir. Me bein' a black guy, I just nat'rally got rhythm. Surely you must've heard.'

'Well, fine.' Missing Obote's scathing sarcasm, Deadman converted his scowl into a smile. 'That's real good of you, Mr Obote.'

'Don't mention it.'

'You're a white man – sorry, poor choice of expression there.'

Deadman hurried off to discover what was keeping his star. In the background he could hear Obote calling, 'Now, listen up, people, and follow me ...'

When he was still twenty yards away from Ann's dressing hut, Deadman could already hear his leading lady's ear-grating voice raised in complaint. 'You tell that lousy crumb Deadman I ain't comin' out, so there!'

Deadman rapped on the door, then clutched at the flimsy bamboo construction before it collapsed. 'Ray! What's going on in there?'

The door opened and Ray's flushed face appeared. 'Oh, Mr Deadman, she won't come out – she says being sacrificed to giant gorillas isn't in her contract.'

'Oh, for Pete's sake.' Deadman took a deep breath and counted to ten. 'OK, Ray, leave this to me. Take five.'

Ray mopped his brow with a highly coloured handkerchief liberally doused with eau de Cologne. 'Thank you, Mr Deadman. If you need me, I'll be having a nervous breakdown.'

Deadman stepped into the hut and found Ann, fully costumed, coiffured and made up, but with her arms folded tightly across her chest and wearing a mulish expression. Deciding that his best option was to humour her, Deadman switched instantly to an attitude of friendly concern. 'What is it, baby?'

'Hah!' Ann shot him a look of pure loathing. 'Like you don't know. You promised me this would be my big break in movies. My name up in lights on every billboard across America. You didn't say nothing about me being sacrificed by a bunch of savages.'

Deadman's voice was as soothing as an old pair of

slippers. 'Listen, toots, I promised you a tall, dark leading man, didn't I?'

'Youse didn't say nothin' about him being no gorilla!'

'So what if he's a little hairy? The way your career's going, you can't be too picky.'

'He's an animal!'

'You've done scenes with Errol Flynn. How could this be worse?'

'He's thirty feet tall!'

'You can stand on a box. All you got to do is scream.'

'You bet I'm gonna scream! I'm gonna scream to my agent, the Screen Actors' Guild …'

'Listen, honey.' Deadman's voice was like the cooing of a turtledove trained in stress counselling. 'You don't have a thing to worry about. All we're shooting today is the scene where you're being prepared for the sacrifice. When it comes to the actual bit where Dong kidnaps you, you won't even be on set! We'll use dummies, body doubles, the whole works. Camera tricks. You get me?' He gave Ann a reassuring wink.

Ann eyed him doubtfully. 'For real?'

'Hey – trust me, I'm a director.'

Ann pouted. 'Well, OK. But this better be on the level.'

'Come on, then.' Deadman checked his watch. 'Obote

should just about have organized the frenzied native dancing by now.' He took Ann by the hand and propelled his disaffected leading lady towards the set.

Deadman placed Ann on her mark and turned to Obote. 'How's the dance coming?'

Obote shrugged and indicated the formation of extras, waiting expectantly for their cue. 'We're ready.'

'Good.' Deadman swung himself into his director's chair. 'Ray, clapperboard, please.'

With a put-upon air, Ray held up the clapperboard. '*A Scary Movie About a Gigantic Dong*, scene thirty-seven, take one.'

'Roll camera,' ordered Deadman, 'and … action!'

Behind the camera, a scratching noise announced that someone had started up a wind-up gramophone and set the needle on the disc. This was followed by the discordant jangle of a dance-band playing 'Yes Sir, That's My Baby'. The extras launched into an energetic Charleston. Knees clamped tightly together, hands sawing the air in counter-rotating circles, feet flicking to the side, buttocks gyrating, the pirates kicked up dust, rolled their eyes, flashed their teeth …

'Cut! Cut!' screamed Deadman. He sprang from his chair and leapt for the gramophone, snatching the needle from the disc with a screech of tortured vinyl. He grabbed a revolver from a grinning sailor and fired it into the air. There was a shocked silence. The dance petered out.

Deadman turned to Obote. '*That's* native dancing?'

'Well, I'm a native of South Carolina, and this is how we dance back in Harlem.'

'I'll deal with you later, wise guy.' Deadman raised his megaphone. 'Like I said, people, I want you shuffling around in a circle and every few seconds you beat your chests, you throw your hands up in the air and you yell, "Dong!" Got that?' The extras, eyes fixed on the revolver that Deadman still held in one dangerously trembling fist, nodded hastily. 'Good.'

The shoot proceeded without further trouble. The extras shuffled round in the approved Hollywood Native Savages Dancing manner. Ann suffered the ministrations of her attendants with no more than an occasional scowl.

Deadman called a wrap, then went to smoke a cigar at the door to Captain Crook's hut while the extras touched up each other's body make-up.

'Ahoy, shipmate.' Crook's throaty voice rumbled from the tent. 'Are we all ready for tonight?'

Deadman took a satisfying drag on his cigar. 'Sure.'

'Miss Darling don't object to being sacrificed?'

'Oh, she objects like anything. Fortunately I have a way of overcoming her scruples.'

'Ooh ar? What be that, matey?'

Deadman grinned. 'Chloroform.'

Ann woke up with a fuzzy head and a raging thirst. She had a vague recollection of some kind of cloth covering her mouth and nose, and a sickly, chemical smell.

Her head began to clear. Blearily, she took stock of her surroundings.

Darkness had fallen. Ann was standing between two gigantic pillars, held in place by ropes cut from jungle vines, which cut cruelly into her wrists. She was wearing her 'virgin sacrifice' costume.

Ann's heart skipped a beat. 'Deadman,' she mumbled through dry lips, 'you lousy fink!'

Before her was a sinister expanse of moonlit jungle. Frantically twisting her head, Ann realized that she was on a platform outside the great gate in the wall, on top of which were gathered the pirates in full native fig, Marzipan, who was biting his nails, and Deadman, who stood shoulder to shoulder with Ray and Captain Crook, turning the handle of his camera.

Ann realized that she was covered in something sticky.

She wriggled uncomfortably. Yuck! Somebody had ... Ann sniffed and stiffened in horror. *Somebody had drenched her from head to foot in banana oil!*

As she stared up at the wall, a brace of brawny pirates began to strike the huge bell that hung above the gates. The sound reverberated across the menacing primeval forest, echoing from the vertiginous cliffs.

DONG ... DONG ... DONG ...

Ann struggled like a maniac. 'Deadman! You creep! I'll get you for this!'

Deadman gave her a big grin and a thumbs-up sign. 'Action!'

Ann screamed the place down.

And all the while, as she struggled and screamed, the great bell continued to send its summons out across the louring jungle.

DONG ... DONG ... DONG ...

CHAPTER ELEVEN

Heeerrre's Dongie!

Indiana Bones was having a bad day.

Everyone had laughed at him. Nobody took him seriously. He was an expert in ancient civilizations and cultures, yet nobody listened to him. Did they think all it took to do his job were a trowel and a map that said 'Dig Here'? These people sure had some strange ideas about archaeology.

And Ann. He had offered her the delicate flower of his love, and she had sprayed it with the weed-killer of her disdain. So he'd decided to go away and live all alone, far from the callous indifference of his fellow-creatures, a poor hermit, a broken-hearted outcast, until he perished from hunger and thirst. And one day Ann would stumble across his pathetic bones, picked clean by the scuttling crabs and the squabbling gulls, and then she'd be sorry.

This comforting reflection had kept him pacing up and down the beach until supper time; at which point insistent pangs of hunger had presented a compelling counter-argument: namely, that Ann probably wouldn't give a tinker's cuss if he perished of hunger and thirst, in fact she'd probably prefer it that way, so he might as well see what was to eat and to hell with her.

Thus it was that Indiana had returned to find the village deserted, the top of the wall lit up with torches, and the sound of a giant bell tolling out across the jungle.

DONG ... DONG ... DONG ...

Big gloopy bubbles of curiosity rose up through the tar-pit of Indiana's self-pity. He mooched through the village and climbed one of the rickety ladders to the top of the wall, where he found all the pirates staring at something way below, just beyond the main gate. Listlessly, he followed their gaze.

His eyes bulged. He grabbed the nearest pirate by the bead necklace and shrieked, 'What are you doing with Miss Darling?'

A few moments later, looking through the camera viewfinder, Deadman stared with growing panic at the approach of a half-crazed, wide-eyed beast, howling and gibbering with primeval animal fury, whose slobbering mouth ballooned to fill his field of vision. The film-maker looked up in shock as Indiana elbowed the camera aside and grabbed him by the throat. 'Deadman, you maniac! Let her go!'

The movie man struggled in Indiana's grip. 'Calm down, Dr Bones!' he rasped. 'What are you getting so het up about?'

'You monster! You're going to sacrifice Ann to Dong!'

'Now then, lad.' Captain Crook signalled and a couple of burly pirates stepped forward to pull Indiana off the choking Deadman. 'Don't get all aerated. It's only for show. It's not like Dong's going to do anythin' to 'er.'

Indiana stared at him. 'How d'you know?' he demanded.

'Because Dong only wants a sacrifice to keep up appearances. Look ...' The Captain patted the incandescent archaeologist comfortingly on the shoulder. ''E comes out of the jungle and bangs his chest a bit, we tremble and shout, *"Dong! Dong!"* and do a bit of bowing and scraping, you know, the old "We are not worthy" routine, 'e seizes her voluptuous, trembling body, ignoring 'er terrified screams, and carries 'er off to 'is jungle lair – and a couple of days later, after Dong and Marzipan have made it up, she sneaks back 'ere without 'im even noticin'. Mr Deadman gets his movie, Dong feels appreciated, everyone's 'appy and no 'arm done.' He turned to the muscled hunk at his side. 'Ain't that right, Marzie?'

'Marzipan not know.' The Lord of the Jungle stopped biting his nails and turned a troubled gaze on Captain Crook. 'Marzipan not like this.'

Indiana pointed a quivering finger at the near-naked ape-man. 'Who the hell is he?'

Crook ignored the question. 'Oh, come off it, Marzie. Me and Wendy have pulled this stunt dozens of times.'

'Marzipan know, but Dong has wised up. Dong in funny mood. Marzipan think Dong use girl to show Marzipan him not only pebble on beach. Marzipan not put it past Dong.'

Captain Crook waved this aside. 'Anyway, lad, she's the Bride of Dong so you may as well get used to it.'

As the debate raged and Deadman struggled to re-set his collapsed camera, Ray stared at Ann's desperate struggles with mounting horror. Her hair was awry, her flower-garlands hung in tatters, her make-up was streaked with tears of fury and terror, her dress was all askew. As Ray stared at the writhing figure, he knew that he could not let this go on. He had to do something.

Slipping away from the pandemonium on top of the wall, Ray found a coil of jungle vine. He knotted the end inexpertly into a loop, which he dropped over a handy projection. He let the vine fall, and slid down it, landing with a thump on the packed earth between wall and jungle.

Winded for a moment, he picked himself up and scuttled to the pillars where Deadman's leading lady struggled fruitlessly against her cruel captivity. 'Ann,' he called, 'Ann.'

Ann stopped screaming and looked around frantically for the source of the voice. At last she spotted her rescuer. 'Ray,' she sobbed, her eyes lighting with hope, 'quick, get me down before Dong comes.'

'Oh baby,' cooed Ray, rummaging in his shoulder-bag, 'what did they do to you?'

'I know, I know, Ray. Cut me down, huh?'

'Look at your hair … your make-up … your dress …'

'Sure, sure, Ray. Could we save the makeover pitch for another time. Just get me the hell outta here, willya?'

'Don't worry, sweetheart, Ray's here.' The costumier brought out a powder compact and a styling brush. 'Can't have you looking like a scarecrow for the cameras, can we?'

'*What?*' Ann struggled with renewed vigour. 'You doity rat, I'll tear ya ta pieces!'

She broke off. An unearthly, appalling, bestial roar split the night air.

The iron tongue of the bell was stilled. Silence descended. Then, as one, the pirates launched into a chorus of celebration and summoning:

'There is nothing like a Dong
Nothing in the world
There is nothing quite as long
As a socking great hairy Dong!'

Captain Crook's incredibly low bass voice added, in tones of awe not untinged with envy:

'There is absolutely nothing that's as long
As his Dong ...'

From deep in the night-shrouded jungle came a powerful, rhythmic thumping, as of the beating of a mighty drum, followed by a bowel-loosening bellow of defiance.

Up on the wall, Deadman stared out over the brooding treescape. The roar came again, louder, even more terrible in its ferocious, inhuman malice. Then, in the middle distance, trees began to quiver and bend. The earth shook to the mighty tread of approaching giant footsteps:

THUMP ... THUMP ... THUMP ...

... nearer and ever nearer.

Deadman was the first to break from the trance. 'Here he comes!' he yelled, grabbing frantically for the camera. 'This is it, boys! This is what we've been – *Ray, what the blazes are you doing down there?*'

Far below, Ray waggled his styling brush.

'Dong's coming, you idiot! Get the hell out of there – oh, shit!' Deadman darted for the camera and began to crank the handle.

Ray looked up. 'Whoops,' he said faintly.

Ann followed his gaze, and let out a scream that left all her previous efforts standing.

Dong had arrived.

Ray and Ann stared in speechless horror. The sight that met their cringing gaze was a monstrous ape-like creature fully thirty feet tall: a foul obscenity, a mind-numbing nightmare, a misbegotten mockery of nature spawned in some unwholesome, aberrant freak of creation.

Her voice trembling with awe, Ann breathed, 'Get a load of that!'

'That is one big monkey,' squeaked Ray.

'Yeah, sure, sure,' said Ann. 'But get a load of *that*!'

Ray tore his eyes away from the horrendous hairy face, and followed her gaze down, to the creature's mighty chest, to its gargantuan belly, still down …

His eyes bulged. His breath caught. He squeaked, 'Oh, my *stars*!'

Eyes still glued to the camera, Deadman gave an appreciative whistle. 'I can see why you call him "Dong".'

Thunderstruck, the crew of the *Vulture* gazed at the gigantic gorilla. Sloppy, the ship's cook, creased his brow in puzzlement. 'You know, there's something strangely familiar about that ape. Can't quite put my finger on it …'

Ann looked Dong up and down. He was kinda hairy, his teeth put her in mind of coastal defences, his eyes shone with bestial savagery, inside his flaring nostrils dangled bogies like beef carcasses, his great gnarled hands were wrinkled like an ancient leather sofa – but boy, was he *hung*!

Her eyes narrowed in speculation. 'Well, hello there, ya big ape.'

Atop the wall, Indiana cupped his hands around his mouth. 'Ann, hang in there! I'll rescue you!'

Ann glared over her shoulder. 'Don't you dare!'

'But he'll carry you off!'

'I can live with it.'

'And take you to his lair deep in the trackless jungle!'

'Sounds good to me.'

'And ravish you unmercifully!'

'I can hardly wait.'

'Chin up, Ann! I'll be right there.'

'Back off, loser!' snapped Ann. 'If it's a choice between you and Dong, call me Mrs Gorilla.'

Indiana was thunderstruck. 'You're kidding! You'd rather go with Dong than with me?' He spread his arms in desperate appeal. 'What's he got that I haven't got?'

Ann gave him a mocking grin. 'Oh, come *on* ...'

'Deadman!' In desperation, Indiana turned to the producer. 'For pity's sake, talk some sense into her!'

'Shaddap, kid.' Deadman continued to crank the camera, his eyes glued to the viewfinder. 'I'm getting some great footage here!'

'Hey, Dongie baby.' Ann fluttered her eyelashes. 'Is that a giant zucchini you're carrying, or are you just pleased to see me?'

Dong leaned closer to Ann and sniffed. 'Gggrrrooooaaawwwwwrrrr?'

'Oh, I bet you say that to all the goils.' Ann gave a sensuous wriggle. 'You're such an animal!'

'Bbbbrrrrooooaaaahhhhh!' Dong reached out with one huge finger.

Ann giggled. 'Hey, knock it off, that tickles!' She tilted her head coquettishly. 'You want we should go back to your place and maybe ... make out a little?'

Heeerrre's Dongie!

'Ggggrrrrrrrrrrrrrrrrrrrrrrrrrrr!'

'Well, watcha waiting for, handsome? Why doncha loosen my bonds ...' Ann lowered her eyes in apparent submission. '... for starters.'

'Rrrrrrrrrrrrrrrrrrrrrrrrrr?'

'And then we can –' Ann's head jerked up. 'Hey! Are you listening to me?'

Something had attracted Dong's attention. The huge creature was no longer looking at his proffered bride. His eyes were directed elsewhere.

On top of the wall, Marzipan groaned. 'Uh-oh!'

'What's 'e doing?' demanded Crook.

Dong had switched his attention from Ann. To the astonishment of the watchers, the huge beast reached down, past its intended bride, and made a grab. Its gigantic hand came back up, holding a slim, struggling, rather effete figure.

Indiana boggled. 'It doesn't want Ann! It's got Fey Ray!'

Deadman stopped cranking and looked up from his viewfinder with an expression of outrage. 'What gives? That ain't in the script!'

Ann's scream of fury wafted up from far below. 'Watcha doin', ya big hairy creep? You scared to tangle with a real woman? Let me down from here, I'll show you.'

139

Dong ignored her. The gigantic ape gazed, enraptured, at Ray. Its tremendous lips curled into an ingratiating leer. It rumbled affectionately, making a noise that sounded for all the world like the words, 'Myyyyyyyyyyyyyyyyyyyy Pppprrrrreeeeeeeeeeeccccccciiiiiiiiiiiioooooouuuuuussssssss.'

Ray gave Dong a faint, terrified smile, said, 'My, aren't you a big boy!', and passed out.

Marzipan let out a heart-rending wail. 'Marzipan cast aside like last year's fashions! Dong two-time Marzipan! Marzipan gave Dong best years of life! Marzipan sorry – make it up with Dong.'

Dong glared at his erstwhile partner. Pursing his huge rubbery lips, the colossal creature blew a raspberry that knocked half a dozen pirates off the wall and raised one enormous digit in an unmistakable gesture.

Marzipan gave a howl of despair. 'Marzipan's mother warned him about apes like Dong! Dong fickle! Marzipan feel used.'

Ann's voice rose to join the complaint. 'Go ahead, run, momma's boy! You're makin' a big mistake, buster! Nobody dumps Ann Darling on a first date and gets away with it.'

Dong ignored both his ex and his intended Bride. The huge beast gave the unconscious Ray a look of tender

140

affection before treating the watchers on the wall to one last bellow of defiance.

Then the giant ape turned his back and, bearing his precious burden aloft in triumph, crashed through the dense trees of the jungle and disappeared into the night.

CHAPTER TWELVE

Beauty and the Beast?

Stomping into the very heart of Skullandcrossbones Island, Dong made his way through the thick jungle vegetation, pushing through the trees and giant plants as though they were stalks of wheat. His journey took him across rivers and yawning ravines, deeper and deeper into the heart of darkness.

By the time Dong reached his destination, it was dawn. The sun's first rays lit his way as the green of the jungle gave way to bare rocky slopes. Grey granite massifs thrust upwards, becoming jagged summits, which intermittently disappeared into rolling banks of mist.

The ape had no time or inclination to admire the view as

he made his way up the slopes, heading for a rocky outcrop, which led to an opening into the mountainside.

Dong stood momentarily at the mouth of this cave, adjusting a wooden sign bearing the message:

No. 1 MOUNTAINSIDE VIEW
No TRADERS. No HAWKERS.
BEWARE of THE GIANT HOMICIDAL GORILLA.

Dong wiped his feet on a WELCOME coconut rush mat the size of a tennis court and entered his lair.

The cave was no small dark refuge. It was cathedral-like, hewn out of the rock over thousands of years by wind and water. A huge lake covered most of the cave floor.

Dong made his way up a natural stone ramp leading to a rocky ledge that ran around the cave wall. Nestled in his mighty paw, Ray began to stir, revived by the colder air. He pulled at the ape's hair as though nestling under a woollen blanket. The creature unfolded his paw, placed Ray gently on the ledge, and began tickling the dresser with his huge forefinger.

The half-asleep Ray began to giggle. 'No, stop it, Rudi, you naughty boy.'

'Groooar?' In an effort to wake the still slumbering

dresser, the ape began pulling at Ray's clothes. His silk shirt came away in Dong's fingers like the white gossamer pappus of a dandelion, to reveal a hairy chest and a gold medallion the size of a tractor hub.

'Errol! You are so nauuuughtyyyyyy!'

Confused, Dong plucked at Ray's trousers.

'Dougie, what *are* you tugging?'

The trousers came away to reveal a pair of Steamboat Willie boxer shorts.

'Ooooooh!'

'Grooaaaarrrrrr!'

Ray jerked awake. Looking up, he gazed into two enormous nostrils. Everything came back to him in an instant. He gave a hoarse cry. Scrambling to his feet, he glanced around frenziedly: at the strange place in which he found himself; at his terrible captor.

'Oh. My. God!' moaned Ray. His mouth worked for a moment, but no sound came out. 'Oh. My. God!' he repeated.

Dong regarded Ray in silence.

'Oh. My. God!' said Ray for a third time. He clapped his hands. 'I just *love* this place! Is this yours?'

Dong nodded.

Ray cast a critical eye. 'Dong, baby, this place has such

potential. I can see what you're trying to do here: the primeval look. Nice. Good use of natural textures – the rock, the vines, the bamboo – they all complement each other. And I like the mezzanine, split-level effect, I do. ' Ray shook his head. 'But it doesn't really gel, does it?'

Dong raised an inquisitive eyebrow. 'Ruuuurrrr?'

'For example.' Ray pointed at the lake below. 'An indoor water feature! Brave, I'll admit, but if you're going to make a statement – be bold!' A dark shape moving swiftly through the water caught Ray's eye. 'Goldfish or koi?'

At that very instant the long neck of a huge water serpent surged up and broke through the lake's surface, its gaping jaws filled with razor-sharp teeth and its tongue flickering as it struck at Ray's unprotected face.

Before Ray could draw breath to scream, Dong reached down and patted the water creature on its head. It gave a low mewl, licked Ray's cheek like an over-familiar puppy, and curled itself lovingly around Dong's forearm before returning to the depths of the lake.

Ray's composure returned. 'OK, it's certainly not coy and it's a teensy weensy bit bigger than a goldfish. Does it have a name?'

'Grrooaor.'

'Nessie? Cute. But it has got to go! I think we're going to

have to make the lake more of a feature – maybe have a fountain? Mind you, that would take a very big pump. But I'm sure you can manage!' Ray gave Dong an outrageous wink. 'We're going to have so much fun …'

Back at the village, Ann was still fuming about Dong's apenapping of Ray. 'I can't believe the big lout preferred the mincer over me! What's Ray got that I ain't?'

'Meat and veg,' said Indiana nastily.

'I don't care,' grouched Ann. 'I got a score to settle with that guy. Like the saying says, "Hell ain't got nothin' over a pissed-off female."'

'You have such a way with words,' muttered Deadman.

'Don't give me that crap!' Ann wagged an angry finger in the producer's face. 'I ain't listenin' to you any more, Deadman. Tryin' a make a monkey outta me – or, more specifically, tryin' to a make a monkey *bride* outta me! And I hate weddings!'

'Huh?' Indiana's ears pricked up. 'You mean – you've been married before?'

'What is this,' demanded Ann, 'a memory test? Listen, Bones, in Hollywood getting married is a good way of spendin' a boring weekend. Hell, the last time I *saw* one of my husbands was at the wedding.'

Beauty and the Beast?

Indiana was shocked. 'Gee, I always thought of marriage as kinda sacred.'

'Give me a break. You get three rings when you marry: engagement ring, wedding ring and suffering.'

'I bet plenty of men 'ave 'ad your ring around their fingers, missy,' leered Captain Crook. The pirates guffawed.

Ann made a certain gesture. 'Up yours, hooky!'

'Will you quit arguing?' demanded Deadman. 'We have to get Ray back.'

'Do we?' asked Ann with genuine puzzlement. 'Why?'

'If we don't, who's gonna do the sewing? Who's gonna wash and iron all the costumes?'

'Oh, I wouldn't worry,' muttered Obote. 'I'm damn sure you'll be able to find some other wage slave to oppress with domestic duties. The man's been carried off to face a terrible death and all you're worried about is your stupid costumes.'

'So you're worried about Ray, Mr Obote?' said Deadman smoothly. 'You think we should mount a rescue attempt?'

'Sure I do!'

'Excellent! Thank you for volunteering.'

'Huh?'

'And obviously your men will want to back you up.'

'Thanks, Obote,' muttered a voice in the darkness. 'You and your mouth.'

'Who else is coming?' demanded Deadman.

'I am!' snapped Ann. 'And when I find that ape I'm gonna give him a piece of my mind.'

'I shouldn't think there was enough of it to share,' muttered Captain Crook.

Indiana leapt to his feet. 'If Miss Darling is going, then I'm going too!'

Ann gave him a jaundiced look. 'My hero,' she said sarcastically. Indiana, oblivious to irony, beamed.

'That's settled, then,' said Deadman. 'We owe it to Ray to journey into the depths of the island, no matter what dangers lie ahead.' The producer rubbed his hands together. 'And just think of the opportunities for filming! A daring rescue! Life-threatening primeval jungle! Hidden terrors! We are gonna have a blockbuster on our hands, even if the rescue doesn't work out ... which it will, of course,' he added hurriedly.

Captain Crook gave a wheezy cough. 'You're forgettin' one thing, lad. There's the little problem of manpower – yer 'aven't got enough men fer such a venture into the dark side.'

Deadman shrugged. 'There's my crew and your pirates.'

Crook broke into a raucous fit of laughter. 'You be jokin', matey! Nothin'll persuade me and my men to join in such a fool'ardy and downright dangerous undertakin'!'

Deadman pulled out a contract from his jacket pocket, unfolded it, and began to read.

'"I, Captain Horatio Ahab Blackbeard Odysseus Crook, do solemnly undertake ..." blah blah blah "... to be responsible for the supply of all film extras, provision of location shooting, and the security of all such persons connected with the making of the film *A Scary Movie About a Gigantic Dong* ..." etcetera, etcetera, and the loss of my dresser sees you in breach of the contract already.'

'And so what?'

Deadman smiled. 'The small print: "Failure to comply with any of the above clauses will result in forfeiture of all film and merchandising rights and the seizure of all personal goods up to the value of $1,000,000." Which would mean you lose everything.'

Crook stared at Deadman with a look that combined loathing and respect. 'Yer more of a pirate than I am, Deadman.'

'That's Hollywood! Let's get moving.'

'Wait a minute!' The Captain held up a restraining hand. 'I'm not going into the depths of no ruddy trackless jungle without a native guide.' He raised his voice and bellowed, 'Oy! Marzipan! Get over 'ere! I got a job fer you!'

After several moments a nearly naked figure stumbled into the firelight. Marzipan's eyes were bleared and his well-muscled body seemed to have gone to flab in the past half hour. He was carrying a gourd. As the others stared at him in dismay, the Lord of the Jungle raised this to his lips and took a hefty swig. He wiped his mouth with the back of his hand, and slurred, 'What Cap'n Crook want with Marzipan?'

Crook seized the gourd and sniffed. 'Kava, by God! The drunken brute must've 'ad 'alf a gallon!'

'Marzipan,' said Deadman in commanding tones. 'We want you to take us to Dong.'

Marzipan shook his head. 'Marzipan no good. Dong dumped Marzipan.' The ape-man's body shook with silent sobs. 'Marzipan wishes he was dead.' The Lord of the Jungle snatched his gourd back from Crook and took another long pull at its contents. Then he collapsed into a sitting position, rocking and cradling the gourd, and singing in a mournful falsetto:

Strumming my pain with his fingers
Singing my life with his words
Killing me softly with his Dong ...'

'Oh, for pity's sake!' snapped Deadman. 'Let's get going before we lose the trail.' He pointed at Marzipan. 'Better

150

bring that drunken bum – maybe he'll be some use when he sobers up.'

The rescue party began to gather, checking weapons and equipment.

Indiana looked across to the great wall and gate, his mind already imagining what horrors might lie beyond. 'Poor Ray,' he whispered. 'God only knows what agonies he's enduring.'

'Noooooo!' Ray shook his head in agony. 'There's too much clutter!' He kicked at a pile of discarded bones littering Dong's cave. 'You're not thinking Feng Shui. We have to allow the space to breathe. Clutter is a boy's worst enemy! We need to sweep this all away so we can release the energy channels.'

'Rrruuuaaaaarrrr!'

'I know, I know. You, Mr Dong, are one just big pent-up blockage of emotion and energy. You need a release.'

'Gruaooorrr?'

Ray's voice became conciliatory. 'I know, I know. That Marzipan doesn't understand you. Well, don't despair, Ray's here and he's known for his expertise in opening up channels.' He reached down and picked up a skull. 'Nice ornament, though, very gothic.'

'Ruuaaarrrrr!'

Ray continued his inventory of Dong's cave, inspecting every wall (mostly covered with Marzipan's crude line drawings) and every hidden recess with careful and considered attention. 'We *are* going to have to do something about the light. It's fundamental to the very nature of a dwelling. We need more daylight, maybe bring in some pastels and don't be too bold.' He gave a shriek. 'You're not *too* bold, are you?'

'Rauauuuuuur!'

'I might not have a Cecil B de Mille budget, but I can do something with this.' He put a finger to his pursed lips. 'We need a style to reflect your personality. What sort of an ape do you see yourself? Would you say you were more Art Deco or Art Nouveau?'

'Rarrrggarrr!'

'Neoclassical, huh?' Ray shook his head sadly. 'That's just so telling! You realize you're cocooning yourself here, away from the world in your quest for isolation and insulation. This cave of yours says so much more about you than you ever could!'

'Grraaarrrrurrr?'

'You're just a big home boy! And I do mean big.' He scrutinized Dong carefully. 'Maybe we could go down the line of rococo with a little bit of Hollywood chintz?' he mused.

Ray's meandering had brought him to a large recess in the cave wall. He peered inside the gloom. He could just make out the outline of a huge wood-framed bed, covered in banana leaves. 'Uh huh! The bedroom – I suppose that's where you and Marzipan ...' Ray gave an involuntary moan and put his hand against the cave wall to steady himself. 'I'm going all limp just thinking about it.' The designer gave a high-pitched squeal of laughter. '... or rather, just the very opposite!'

Captain Crook gave his head a worried shake. 'We're lost.'

'How can that be?' demanded Deadman. 'We've hardly been travelling an hour.'

'Easily done,' said Indiana. 'Have you noticed how every bit of this jungle looks just like every other bit?'

'Budget constraints, lad, leading to limited sets.' Crook turned to his 'native guide'. 'Marzipan, where are we?'

Marzipan, who was being supported by two grim-faced pirates, looked up dully. 'Marzipan not know. Marzipan useless. Don't ask Marzipan.'

'Dammit, you must know! You've been this way hundreds of times.'

'Marzipan swing on vines. On ground, Marzipan can't tell one tree trunk from another.'

Obote's cantankerous voice muttered, 'Anyway, I don't see why I should be puttin' my ass on the line for no damn lie-around honky just 'cause nobody else know how to use a sewin' machine.'

'OK,' said Deadman, taking charge of the situation. 'We need to spread out, see if we can find some tracks – I mean, jeez, how can a great hulking ape be difficult to follow?'

A voice at his feet said, 'I think I found a footprint.'

'Well done, Dr Bones! How did you do that?'

'I fell in it.'

Deadman bent down and helped the struggling archaeologist climb out of a water-filled footprint the size of a backyard swimming pool. 'Well, at least we know we're on his trail. Come on!'

The party set off again, hacking and slashing their way through the thick jungle vegetation.

Almost at once they encountered a strange, noxious smell. Several of the party began to retch. Then the flies appeared, buzzing and droning in their thousands. Beating them away did little good – for every fly swatted a dozen or so replaced it. They staggered forward, almost blind.

Beauty and the Beast?

The ground began to ooze underfoot.

'I think we've found ourselves a swamp,' yelled Crook, swatting ineffectually at the flies with his hook.

'I don't think so.' Deadman called a halt, and pointed to a monstrous steaming mound. 'We're on the right track.'

'You mean,' said Ann faintly, 'that's Dong's dung?'

Indiana nodded wisely. 'Us jungle trackers would call it his spoor.'

'Us goils from Brooklyn would call it his –'

'Marzipan did say Dong go ape-shit.' Marzipan keeled over in a drunken heap and began to snore.

'Oh, leave him!' snapped Deadman. Holding his nose, he led the party past the steaming heaps, and further into the jungle.

Another hour of backbreaking toil passed before Deadman pulled up suddenly. The others made their way forward to see what had caused their leader to stop.

A gigantic shadow loomed on the trail ahead. There was a sound of trees breaking like matchsticks. As the rescue party watched in awe, the animal casting the shadow stepped forward into a shaft of sunlight.

'Holy mother of ... It can't be!' cried Indiana. 'Those creatures have been dead for millions of years!'

The others stood stock still, jaws and sphincters open wide.

In the clearing in front of them stood the monstrous figure of a Tyrannosaurus Rex.

CHAPTER THIRTEEN

Gorilla Warfare

The rescue party stood rooted to the spot in shock. The T Rex cocked its monstrous head to one side and eyed them beadily.

Indiana grabbed Ann by both arms. 'Ann! Don't go near it!'

'You got any more blindingly obvious advice?' demanded Ann. 'Such as "Do not lie down on the railroad tracks" or "Never go to a Mob meeting and say, 'Hi, I'm Elliot Ness. I'm unarmed and nobody knows I'm here.'"'

Only Deadman seemed undaunted. He punched the air. 'Yes! Oh, yes! This is fantastic!'

'What?' Obote turned a haggard face towards his employer.

Deadman was feverishly setting up his camera. 'I've got to take some shots of that crittur. This is the kind of footage you just can't get without nine months of working with those screwballs in stop-motion. Look at that thing move!'

'Oh, I'm lookin' at it,' averred Obote in a quavering voice, 'and what I mostly observe is that it's moving towards us!'

The rescue party raised their guns to the firing position and began a slow retreat.

'I told yer, lads!' Captain Crook's voice was balanced precariously between triumph and terror. 'I told yer, didn't I? Bloody great newts, I said.'

'I thought you were talking about something like an iguana,' said Deadman, wrestling with the camera mount, 'or maybe a Komodo dragon: nothing like this! This is gonna be a picture to die for!'

Obote gulped. 'That's what I'm afraid of!'

The T Rex roared. It sounded like a dozen tigers with their tails caught in a door. The guns wavered.

Deadman had finally got the camera set up. 'OK, boys. When I turn the camera, I want you to pretend to be terrified, and run away.'

'Pretend?' roared Crook.

'Hey,' complained Obote, 'we signed on as ship's hands. You never said nothin' about us appearing as extras in your movie, which will cost you extra in accordance with standard SAG negotiated rates ...'

The T Rex roared again, and charged.

'... but I'm sure we can work out the details later,' added Obote hurriedly. 'Under the circumstances, I think we can dispense with a card ballot, and move to a resolution on the indication of a simple majority. All those in favour of appearing as extras in Mr Deadman's movie by running away indicate by screaming, "Aaaaaarrrrggghhhh!"'

'Aaaaaarrrrggghhhh!' screamed the rescue party to a man, dropping their weapons.

'All those against? Any abstentions? The ayes have it. All yours, Mr Deadman.'

The rescue party took to its heels in a shrieking, panic-stricken rout.

'You're supposed to wait till I yell "Action!",' objected Deadman. 'Oh, what the hell.' He turned the camera, panning swiftly to follow the ferocious thunder-lizard as it lumbered in pursuit of his men. 'You at the back there! What's your name! Kowalski! Slow down a little. Let him catch up to you. That's it! Tripping over that tree root, good thinking, great improv! Now, as he bends over you,

159

scream! That's it! Keep that expression of horror as he chomps you in half! Great!' Deadman raised his voice. 'Hey, you men! Lead the creature back in a circle, towards the camera!'

From the depths of a jungle, a disembodied voice that might have been Obote's echoed faintly: 'Like buggery we will!'

Indiana peeked out from the bush into which he had taken a flying leap on the dinosaur's initial charge. 'You think we should go help those guys?'

Ann's tousled head appeared through a gap in the leaves to his right. 'They look like they're having fun. Let's vamoooose.'

Indiana bit his lip. 'I dunno. A rugged action hero would –'

'– never dream of leaving a poor defenceless goil all alone in a dangerous jungle. Would he?' On her first view of Skullandcrossbones Island's extravagantly toothy wildlife, Ann had instantly concluded that she needed Indiana to help her get back to the village, in the same way that a farmer crossing a minefield needed a goat on the end of a piece of string – a *long* piece of string – to go first.

Indiana preened. 'Well, when you put it that way …'

The intrepid explorer and Dong's unwanted bride

backed slowly through the undergrowth, and slipped away.

'Don't worry,' said Indiana. 'I'm an expert in jungle survival. If anyone can get us out of this, I can.'

'Is that a fact?' Ann looked far from convinced.

'Sure! I've been roaming around jungles all my life. I can build a fire in a swamp. I can tell you which plants are safe to eat, and which are deadly poisons.'

'Yeah?' Ann was grudgingly impressed. 'That's some skill.'

'Just a knack,' said Indiana airily. 'I'm well known for my bushcraft.'

'I find that hard to believe,' drawled Ann. 'If you've ever been near a bush, I'll be a monkey's uncle.'

Oblivious to Ann's sarcasm, Indiana continued, 'I can show you which leaves to chew as an antidote if you get stung by a scorpion or bitten by a venomous spider.'

'Do you know which leaves to chew if you're bitten by a king cobra?'

Indiana gave a patronising chuckle. 'Silly girl. There is no antidote to the bite of a king cobra. All you can do is write to your loved ones to say "Goodbye" and "No flowers by request". Why do you ask?'

'Because there's one crawling up your pants leg.'

Indiana's screams matched those of the luckless Kowalski.

High in his jungle lair, Dong heard the roars of the enraged Tyrannosaurus and the shrieks of Ray's would-be rescuers. He gave an interrogative grunt. 'Uuuurrrggghhh?'

Ray made a face. 'Are you paying attention?'

It was difficult for a thirty-foot ape to look contrite, but Dong managed it. 'Aaarrrooooaaawww?'

'No, we have not finished. And we're not going to finish if you keep letting yourself be distracted by every little noise.' Ray smoothed down his hastily improvised samples in a marked manner. 'Now, the floor. Do you like the palm-leaf pattern, or the jungle flowers? Personally, I prefer the jungle flowers because –'

The noises came again. Dong roared in reply, and beat his mighty chest with his clenched fists.

'Oh, typical!' Ray tossed his head. 'This relationship is all you, you, you! Every time I try to talk to you about something that interests *me*, all you want to do is goof off and run around with the boys. Well, go on then, I'll just have to choose the new colour scheme for the cave myself.' Dong bounded from his rocky *pied-à-terre* with Ray's shrill complaint ringing in his ears. 'But if you don't like it when it's done, don't you dare come crying to me!'

Ann snatched the machete from Indiana's nerveless fingers. 'Give me that! And unbutton your flies.'

Indiana gave a low moan. 'Ann, you know I find you really attractive, but do you really think this is the time for –'

'Keep still, dummy! It probably thinks you're a shady branch or something. If you loosen your pants, it'll keep going up. All I got to do is wait until it pokes its head out and ...' She brandished the machete in a threatening manner. '... chop!'

'Right.' Indiana licked his lips. In a choked voice, he said, 'Ann ...'

Ann was watching his crotch like a cat at a mouse hole. 'What?'

'If you see something poking out down there ... before you ... chop ...' Indiana swallowed hard. 'Do me a favour, huh? Just make damned sure it's the snake!'

'OK, OK! Don't get excited.'

'Believe me, I'm trying very hard not to.'

Deadman peered into the jungle. It didn't look like the rescue party were coming back. He scowled. That was the movies all over! The minute things started to get the slightest bit risky, everyone started pointing out safety clauses in their contracts and yelling for their stunt doubles.

He cupped his hands around his mouth. 'Hey, you guys! What's the point of me standing here with the camera when all the action is happening over there?'

For a moment there was no reply, then once again Deadman heard screams – but this time approaching his position. Seconds later the surviving members of the *Vulture*'s crew burst into view. Though staggering with exhaustion, they put on a creditable burst of speed, glancing over their shoulders as they ran, and letting out involuntary shrieks of pure, unadulterated terror.

Deadman leapt for the camera. 'That's more like it! OK, I want you to run to my left, as if Dong himself was after you – hey, whaddaya know? Dong *is* after you! OK, you run, you're terrified, you keep falling over for no readily apparent reason, you keep looking back at the murderous beast following you. Great screaming! Now what are you stopping for?' Deadman looked up momentarily from his camera, and his face split into an insane grin. 'Oh, I get it. The T Rex has doubled back to cut you off!'

Indeed, the T Rex had stepped out of the jungle in the path of the terrified men, blocking their retreat.

'Neat move. OK, men! You run from the T Rex – but Dong's there! You run from Dong – but the T Rex is there! T Rex – Dong. Dong – T Rex. Running into each other in panic, that's good. Now huddle all together in abject terror.'

'Steady, men.' Obote tried to back through the dense knot of panic-stricken sailors who were determinedly shoving him to the front of the group. 'Look! Dong's seen the T Rex, the T Rex sees Dong. With any luck they'll start fighting each other, and we can slip away.'

The T Rex lifted its head and bellowed defiance. Dong bellowed back, his huge, hairy face twisted into a bestial scowl. The two great creatures came together, circling warily. They approached each other until they were standing eyeball to eyeball. Then Dong raised one great fist – and cupped it round his mouth.

The petrified sailors looked on in stupefaction. 'What gives?' asked one.

The T Rex cocked its head to bring one giant reptilian ear close to Dong's hand.

'Looks like he's whispering something,' said another sailor.

The first nodded. 'To the T Rex. Was that a *snicker*?'

The T Rex moved round behind Dong, who loomed over the hapless *Vulture* crew and dropped into a crouch, legs akimbo, one set of knuckles pressed down into the forest floor. The great ape let out a series of grunts that sounded for all the world like, 'Niiinnneteeeen, Fooouuurrrtty Eeeiigghhhtt, Thhhiiiirrrttttyyyy Tttwwwoooo, Hup!'

On the last grunt the colossal beast scooped up the howling Obote and flung him between his outstretched legs to the T Rex, which braced itself and swung its muscular tail round in a powerful arc, connecting with Obote's flailing body and sending it crashing into the trees.

Dong and the T Rex whooped and exchanged high-fives.

'They're not gonna fight!' shrieked a surviving sailor who had just realized that his continuing survival was likely to be of very limited duration. 'They're helping each other. Aaaaaarrrggghhhhh!' he added, as Dong hurled him the length of the clearing to be caught on the fly by the T Rex, who slammed him head first into the turf – thus proving the accuracy of his prediction – and returned to Dong for another round of hand-slaps.

'Touchdown!' yelled one of the sailors. His nearest neighbours beat the bejasus out of him.

The boatswain yelled blue murder as Dong snatched him from the edge of the group – then paused, mouth open in astonishment as Dong, instead of biting his head off, lay down flat on his belly, and steadied the boatswain in a standing position with one huge finger placed on the trembling man's head.

'Uh-oh,' said the football fan. 'Field goal attempt.'

The boatswain's eyes widened as the significance of the remark shot home, and he opened his mouth to yell – just as a huge punt from the T Rex sent him sailing between two tall trees, to disappear with a final-sounding crash into the dense jungle beyond.

The two terrors of the jungle finished congratulating each other on their latest successful play, and turned, grinning horribly, to face the cringing remnants of the rescue party.

The football aficionado clasped his hands together above his head and gave the looming titans an ingratiating leer.

'Time out?' he inquired, without much hope.

In another part of the jungle, at the edge of the trackless swamp by which he and his men had prudently taken refuge from the marauding Tyrannosaurus, Captain Crook peered around the trunk of a tree. He sniffed the air and listened carefully. Then he stepped cautiously out of cover, and beckoned. 'All clear, lads.'

The pirates appeared from hiding places all around the clearing.

Crook absent-mindedly scratched his nose with his hook. 'Ow!' Using his handkerchief to stem the bleeding, the pirate captain continued, 'Well, lads, we're well out o' that.

Them poor fellas from Mr Deadman's crew never stood a chance. A shame, but there it is. It's no skin off my nose. *Don't nobody make any smart remarks or they'll be very sorry!* Now what say we forget this rescue malarkey and nip back to the village smartish before that little sod Pan shows up.'

He gave a howl as a well-placed catapult shot struck his ample rump. He spun round.

Pan was standing on thin air, arms folded, legs akimbo. The flying urchin gave Captain Crook a satirical glance. 'Too late, Captain. That little sod Pan *has* shown up. And I've brought some friends.'

Pan gave a piercing whistle. The bushes to the north rustled. Out stepped a score or so of sneering louts carrying crudely fashioned baseball bats and motorcycle chains, and wearing offensive T-shirts, torn leathers, and boots specifically banned by the terms of the Geneva Convention.

Pan whistled again. The bushes to the south parted to reveal a stony-faced Red Indian squaw, surrounded by a couple of dozen painted and befeathered braves, all wearing vicious scowls and buckskins, and armed to the teeth.

Captain Crook breathed, 'Oh, bollocks!'

Then he stiffened, eyes rolling, as a new sound emanated

from the depths of the swamp at his rear, a quiet, almost restful sound that nevertheless filled the hardened rogue with bowel-loosening dread.

'Tell me, Captain Codfish,' said Pan in mocking tones, 'can you hear something … ticking?'

CHAPTER FOURTEEN

Plots and Pans

'Good call, man!'

'Shut up and run!'

'I mean, great idea! "Time out"! Inspired.'

'How was I to know they'd bring on their substitutes?'

The remnants of the *Vulture*'s crew crashed through the jungle. They had passed beyond terror into a state of dull shock in which their numbed legs kept going as a purely automatic reaction to the deadly pursuit from which they fled.

Behind them raced an offensive line comprising an iguanadon, a hadrosaurus and four velociraptors, all gnashing their teeth and calling to each other gleefully as they ran. Tucked in behind were an armoured ankylosaurus, a triceratops and a stegosaurus. These in turn were followed by a diplodocus and an apatosaurus in the fullback positions, lumbering gamely along in the hope that when their more agile cousins had had their fun there would still be survivors to be stamped on and squished.

On a small rise overlooking the scene, Deadman turned the camera. Inside, he bubbled with unholy glee. This footage would make him a dozen fortunes. 'Great action scene!' he cried. 'Rogers, climb that tree! That's it, right to the top! Oh, that velociraptor almost had you! But you're beyond its reach, even the iguanadon can't get at you there – oh, here comes the apatosaurus. That's it! Great screaming! Now, it's going to pluck you off that high branch like a ripe piece of fruit – oh, come on, you call that squirming? You can do better than that. That's more like it. One last agonised look at the camera – and cut! Into several pieces, as it happens.'

Indiana and Ann stood at a fork in the jungle track they'd been following, debating which way to take.

'Quit stallin', Bones,' snapped Ann. 'I need to get back to the village. My hair is a mess, my dress is a rag and I think I split a fingernail.'

Indiana looked troubled. 'I can't help feeling we've left the other guys in the lurch. We shouldn't be running away like this.'

Ann gave an inward sigh and decided she'd better humour the sap. 'We are not running away,' she said persuasively. 'This is a strategic withdrawal, and I should know. I've experienced more withdrawals than you've had hot dinners.'

'I guess we could return to the village and gather together another group of rescuers,' said Indiana reluctantly.

'Sure, sure … but we gotta be realistic. Let's face it, Bones. Ray's a gonner.' A smile lit up Ann's face. 'Hey, it's true what they say – every cloud *does* have a silver lining! Anyway, let's get back pronto. We can discuss the rescue bit later.'

'So which path should we take?' mused Indiana. 'The left or right one?'

'Left,' said Ann.

Indiana gave a condescending chuckle. 'Miss Darling, I think you should leave this decision to me. After all, I am the bushcraft expert. You need to try and see things from my point of view.'

'I couldn't get my head so far up my ass,' snapped Ann. 'I'm telling you, Bones, we need to go left.'

Indiana smiled. 'You shouldn't jump to conclusions – bushcraft means reading the little tell-tale signs.' He bent down and rubbed his hand on the ground. 'Now here's a clue. The ground is more solid on the right fork – which suggests it's a more travelled route, which leads me to conclude that the village is that way.' Pleased with himself, he stood up. 'Let's see what other signs we can find to confirm this.'

'We need to go left,' repeated Ann, as Indiana made his way to a tree and carefully inspected it.

The explorer gave a delighted chuckle. 'Another little sign! Fungi grows on the north-facing side of tree trunks. The left fork trees have the fungi growing on the pathwards side of the trunk. The village is south, so it's the right fork we need. See what I mean? Little simple things.'

'You're the little simple thing!' yelled Ann. 'We gotta go left.'

Indiana looked hurt. 'And why do you think that when all the evidence points to the right fork?'

'Because the little tell-tale sign says so!' Ann grabbed hold of Indiana and shoved him towards a painted wooden sign nailed to a tree.

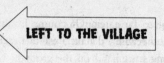

LEFT TO THE VILLAGE

Indiana gave an embarrassed cough. 'I think we should go left.'

Elsewhere in the jungle, Deadman hauled his awkward camera tripod through the clutching undergrowth. He had plenty of shots; now his priority was to get back to the village and make sure the film was properly sealed and stowed in case some terrible accident should destroy the fruits of his labour.

'Mr Deadman!' The croaking voice halted the movie man in his tracks. He looked from side to side and saw a dark hand beckoning from a bush.

Deadman parted the leaves and stared at the figure lying in the inadequate shelter. 'Obote! Is that you?'

'Well, it ain't Al Freakin' Jolson!'

'You look like shit.'

'No kidding? I just been used for batting practice by a goddamn Tyrannosaurus. How the hell d'you expect me to look?'

Deadman tut-tutted. 'Can you walk?'

'Sure, only I prefer lying around in a dinosaur-infested

jungle waiting to be eaten. Of course I can't walk, you numbskull – otherwise I'd have busted myself out of this freak show long since.'

Deadman patted the injured man on the shoulder. 'Don't worry. I'll go back to the village and get help.'

Obote clutched fitfully at Deadman's torn jacket. 'No you don't! No you don't! Don't you go leavin' me!'

'But if you can't walk …' protested Deadman.

'Oh, no! I know how this goes! I seen it in the movies a million times! When there's a black guy and a white guy together, the black guy always gets sick, or shot, or bitten by a rattlesnake or whatever, and the white guy says he'll stay with him no matter what, but does he? Nosiree, because the black guy always spouts some bullshit like, "No, man, you got a wife and kids to consider," or "I'll be fine! Go on without me!", so the white guy looks all manly and concerned but that's just for show 'cause in the end he gets his sorry white ass the hell out of there anyway, and then the black guy dies. Every damn time!'

'Look, Obote,' objected Deadman, 'I can't carry you out of here. I'm already carrying the camera.'

'Then put the camera down, man! What is more important to you, the suffering of a fellow creature or that damn camera?'

There was a brief silence. Then Deadman stooped to pick up his unresisting burden.

'Hey, man, where you goin'? I said *put down* the camera, man! That was supposed to be an appeal to your conscience! Oh, fine. White guy walks away, black guy gonna die, *again*. What'd I tell you?' There was a rustling in the bushes behind Deadman. He didn't look back. Obote's accusing voice wafted up the track. 'Oh, here come the giant spiders! Right on cue. They as big as Packards an' all hairy an' they got more eyes than a sack o' potatoes and green ichor drippin' from their mandibles. What did I say? What did I say? I told you the black guy always dies in these – *Aaaaaarrrrrrgggggggghhh!*'

Deadman paused and looked back at the threshing bushes. He shook his head and muttered, 'What a weiner.'

Then he hefted the camera on his shoulder and headed off down the track towards the village.

The surviving members of the *Vulture*'s crew crept through the jungle in a straggling line, trying desperately not to disturb a single leaf that, by its shaking, might reveal their presence.

Eventually the leader of the line called a halt. He peered carefully along the track ahead. 'It looks clear up there,' he whispered to the man immediately behind him. 'We seem to have shaken off the dinosaurs, and I think we lost Dong. Pass it on.'

The second man in line turned to the third. 'We shook off the dinos, and I think we lost Dong. Pass it on.'

The message passed down the line. 'I think we lost Dong. Pass it on.'

'I think we lost Dong. Pass it on.'

'I think we lost Dong. Pass it on.'

The sixth man in line turned to the shadowy figure standing behind him. 'I think we lost Dong. Pass it on.'

'Oooh iiiigggnnn ooooh osss Ooooonnnngg. Goottcchhhaaa.'

The sixth man looked up into the giant hairy grinning face looming above him. 'Aaaaaaaaaarrrrrrggggggggggg-hhhhhhhhhhh!'

The terrified sailors ran for their lives. Bellowing happily, Dong knuckled along behind them.

Captain Crook twisted his unwholesome face into the semblance of an ingratiating grin. 'Now, me old mate,' he wheedled, 'you and me 'as always got on, 'aven't we?'

Pan raised an ironic eyebrow. 'Refresh my memory. When?'

'Oh, well, we've 'ad our ups and downs, I daresay. I've tried to spit you on the end of my 'ook, you've set fire to my trousis, but it was all in fun, weren't it? I mean, you wouldn't really want ter see old Captain Crook swallered 'ole by a nasty tickin' crocodown-dilly, would ye? That 'orrible beast's trying ter murder me in cold blood!'

'Well, he is a reptile.'

'Come on, matey. Ain't there some other way o' settlin' our triflin' differences?'

Pan appeared to consider this. 'Maybe there is.' The hovering delinquent indicated a broad leaf on which reclined a tiny figure: a girl, no more than three inches from head to foot, with gossamer wings, glowing with fairy dust. The small creature appeared to be ill. It attempted to rise – but then fell back, exhausted.

'Tinklebell is very sick,' said Pan mournfully. 'I'm afraid she will die because people don't believe in fairies any more. But I'm sure *you* believe in fairies, don't you, Captain?'

Hastily, Captain Crook nodded.

'And what about your men? Do they believe in fairies?'

There was an affirmative chorus of 'Aah-harr's and 'Ooo-arrr's.

Pan gave Crook an evil grin. 'Then to make Tinklebell feel better you must show that you believe in fairies. And you can do that by clapping your hands. All right, Captain?'

'Why, you little ...' Crook choked down the biting response that had risen, unbidden, to his lips. He contorted his features into a ghastly smile. 'Whatever yer say, old son.'

'Well then?'

Hook clapped. 'Ow!' He stared at the hook embedded in his palm.

Pan grinned. 'And you have to say,' he continued, 'I do believe in fairies, I do, I do, I *do* believe in fairies!'

'I ... I ...' Crook steeled himself. 'I do believe in fairies, I do, I do, I *do* believe in fairies!' There were snickers behind him. The Captain glared over his shoulder. 'Clap, you swabs!'

One by one, the pirates joined in with the applause, and set up a guttural chorus of, 'I do believe in fairies, I do, I do, I *do* believe in fairies!'

The applause seemed to revive Tinklebell. At least, after several false starts (during which the applause died away and, at a glare from Pan, picked up again), she fluttered her wings, rose into the air and, leaving a contrail of fairy dust, flew to hover at Pan's shoulder.

Very softly, Pan said, 'And what are you, Captain?'

Captain Crook seethed inwardly. But the ticking was still behind him, getting nearer and nearer. Gritting his teeth, he muttered, 'I'm a codfish.'

Pan cupped his ear with his hand in a theatrical gesture. 'I can't hear you!'

Bated beyond endurance, Crook bellowed, 'I'm a codfish!'

'I thought you were.' Pan's face twisted into a snarl of pure malice. 'Get them!'

The scene instantly exploded into action. From one direction, the Lost Boys, baseball bats, chains and boots swinging, descended on the hapless pirates. From the other, with savage war-whoops, Tiger Lilly and her braves rushed to the attack. Their tomahawks rose and fell. Suddenly tonsured pirates ran screaming from the Red Indians only to fall beneath the flailing steel toecaps of the Lost Boys.

Crook stepped back, aghast, from the mêlée – and belatedly realized that he was now ankle-deep in the swamp. Horror welled up in him with the swiftness of fluid in a hydraulic pump. He turned just in time to see a V-shaped ripple arrow through the still water, directly towards him – and suddenly the Captain's vision was full of a writing green body and gaping man-trap jaws as his scaly nemesis rocketed from the water in an explosion of spray and swallowed the shrieking pirate captain between a *TICK* and a *TOCK*.

CHAPTER FIFTEEN

Do Drop In

Deadman's mind was on fire. Even in his wildest dreams he'd never imagined that this whole expedition would have turned out so well. What a movie this was going to be! He'd wipe the floor with the Academy awards! Best Film, Best Director! Hell, even Ann might win a statue – her screaming had been something else. Carl Deadman was going to become the biggest name in the movie business – and what about the money? He felt giddy just thinking about it. OK, there was a downside – Ray was missing, lost in action (but what action!), and Ann was heaven knows where, but blondes in Hollywood (natural and unnatural) were ten a dime. And if she didn't turn up, well, he'd make a saving on her salary! She could receive her award posthumously! He was in a win-win situation, whichever way you looked at it.

Lost in his thoughts, Deadman didn't see the outstretched figure of Marzipan lying on the ground.

'What the …!' Deadman tripped over the supine Lord of the Jungle and went flying. Holding tightly on to the precious camera he hit a tree and crashed to the ground. Frantically, Deadman checked the photographic equipment and breathed a deep sigh of relief. His precious cargo was safe! The producer made his way over to Marzipan and gave him a kick to show how relieved he was. 'You damn idiot! I could have been hurt!' He gave him another kick for luck.

Marzipan stirred and rubbed at his head. 'Marzipan feel like big gorilla crap in his mouth.'

'I don't wanna know what you and Dong get up to. Serves you right for necking that Kava.'

Marzipan got to his feet. 'Marzipan unhappy. Marzipan not think Dong love him any more. Marzipan realize that relationships change as partners develop different needs and aspirations, and this can lead to friction. Marzipan aware that skilled counselling can help both parties find a way forward, but if all attempts at mediation fail, it time to let go and move on.'

King Dong

Deadman stared. 'What the hell are you talking about?'

'Marzipan must set aspirations lower. Maybe meet chimpanzee, maybe one confusingly named after member of cat family, and start producing little monkeys.'

'I like it!' Deadman's business brain clicked in. 'What a pitch! It's the classic tale – boy meets ape, boy spurned by ape, boy meets another ape – love is the winner. Or maybe a screwball comedy drama! Hey, Marzie, can I have the film rights? I'll make you an executive producer! Maybe get Johnny Weissmuller to play you – no, he's a swimmer, not an actor, that would be ridiculous, don't mind me, I'm wandering.' He clasped his camera to his chest and grabbed hold of Marzipan's arm. 'Come on, Marzie, we've gotta get back to the village. Dong's on the rampage, Lord knows what's happened to Ray – or Ann and Indiana, come to that. Crook and his men have disappeared and my boys are out there somewhere playing hide-and-seek with a bunch of homicidal dinosaurs. Something tells me that this situation is gonna get a whole lot worse before it gets better.'

'Have they given up?'

The pirates, panting, staggered to a halt and listened. The sounds of pursuit seemed to have faded.

184

'We've lost them,' said one. 'Lost the Lost Boys.' He gave a feeble giggle.

'That's real funny,' a colleague told him. 'That's a riot.'

'Hi there.'

The pirates stared as a small group of strangers wandered into the clearing from the opposite direction. In the lead was a middle-aged man with frown lines round his eyes and receding, swept-back hair, wearing a blue shirt and a red neckerchief. He was carrying a small boy whose frizzed-out hair and smouldering clothes made him look as if he'd just received a jolt of at least 100,000 volts. Behind them trotted a small girl wearing mud-encrusted clothes and a stunned expression.

The man gave the pirates a jaundiced look. 'Don't ask,' he said. 'It's just been one bitch of a day.'

The pirates exchanged glances. 'You 'aven't seen Dong anywhere around here?' asked one.

The man raised an eyebrow. 'Dong?' He looked put out. 'This isn't Triassic Park?' The pirates shook their heads. 'Looks like we wandered into the wrong parody.' The man set off downslope, calling over his shoulder, 'But if you see a white-haired old bugger who walks with a stick, tell him I've got a bone to pick with him. Mucking about with dinosaur DNA! Talk about asking for trouble.'

As the man disappeared from view, the pirates heard a voice that turned their blood to ice. 'Guess who?'

The pirates screamed as one as the Lost Boys appeared and moved in for the final kill.

Ray stepped back and surveyed the cave with a look of satisfaction.

All his hard work had been well worth it. The shag pile carpet had taken a bit of hunting up on a desert island, but it did a lot to level the uneven floor. The water feature was fountaining nicely, the chiffon drapes really *worked*, and he was pleased with the distressed marbling effect on the walls. They set off the flower garlands very nicely, and the bamboo screens really broke up the space. He couldn't imagine how he'd ever got it all done in so little time!

He hoped Dong would be pleased.

Back in the jungle, despite earlier setbacks, Indiana was still giving Ann the benefit of his experience in bushcraft. Ann was giving Indiana the benefit of her experience of ignoring jerks.

'The jungle is an unforgiving environment. You have to be aware of every possibility of danger. Be alert and awake at all times.'

Ann yawned.

Indiana pushed through the thick vegetation. 'Every step you take could be your last. Lucky you've got me, to show you the ropes and guide you and – AARGGGHH!'

Indiana crashed downwards and disappeared from sight.

'Stop jerkin' around, Bones!'

A plaintive cry of 'Help!' drifted from the spot Indiana had fallen.

Sighing heavily, Ann stepped forward and nearly stumbled. She staggered back, realizing why Indiana had disappeared so suddenly. They were on the edge of a ravine.

'Help!'

Ann dropped to her knees and crept forward. She looked over the edge of the precipice. Below her, Indiana was swinging in the void, hanging on grimly to the jungle vine that had saved his life.

'Don't let go!' said Ann.

'Now who's giving out the obvious advice!' screamed Indiana. 'Get me outta here!'

'Say "please".'

'What?'

'Say "please".'

'Please.'

'Say "And if you do rescue me I'll stop bugging you."'

'Are you crazy! I could die!'

'Looks that way. So you'd better say it. Now!'

'And if you do rescue me I'll stop bugging you.'

'Good!'

Ann wrapped another vine around her waist and tied it to a tree. She then reached over the edge of the drop and grabbed hold of the vine to which Indiana was clinging. With a great deal of grunting and groaning, she managed to haul the acrophobic archaeologist up from the abyss.

'You saved my life,' gasped Indiana.

'Everyone makes mistakes. Don't hold it against me.'

Indiana glanced at the vine tied to Ann. 'Tying yourself to a tree! Where did you get that idea?'

'Let's just say I'm an expert on certain types of bushcraft.' As Ann untangled the vine, Indiana studied the yawning gap that had halted their progress. Sheer rock faces plummeted downwards. Indiana shook his head mournfully. 'It's not the Grand Canyon, but it's enough to stop us. We'll have to head back the way we came. It's going to take time and it's going to be dangerous – we'll have to make sure we avoid Dong and the dinosaurs. Don't be scared, Ann. I'm used to getting out of tight spots. It's going to be a long haul, but with luck we could make it back to the village before nightfall.'

'Or we could just cross that bridge over there.'

Indiana looked to where Ann was pointing. A huge tree trunk lay across the ravine, thirty yards away.

'Ah, yes – a wooden bridge. I thought there might be one of those about. Well spotted. Good.'

Muttering, Ann headed for the bridge, Indiana in her wake. She had nothing against bottomless ravines as such, she just wasn't crazy about the idea of crossing one – and if she had to cross it she'd prefer to do so on something a little more secure-looking – for instance, the Brooklyn Bridge. But the only alternative seemed to be a fun night out in a jungle full of monsters … Crossing her fingers, Ann stepped onto the log.

Actually, the journey across wasn't too bad. The log was wide and the rough bark gave good grip, so walking across it was reasonably easy.

'Don't look down,' warned Indiana.

'Why does everyone say that in these situations?' demanded Ann peevishly. 'Why the hell should I look down, when I'm going forward? Aah!'

'What happened?'

'I looked down!'

'Why did you look down? I told you not to look down.'

'I only looked down because you told me not to look

down! If you hadn't told me not to look down, I wouldn't
have looked down!'

Recovering from her momentary attack of vertigo, Ann
led the way along the trunk, carefully manoeuvring over
knots and jutting branches. With a gasp of relief, she
stepped off the trunk onto terra firma. Moments later,
Indiana followed.

Immediately the jungle air was filled with bestial roars,
and human shouts and screams.

Ann peered across the ravine. 'Over there!'

In an explosion of movement, the remaining members
of the crew appeared from the jungle foliage. The
men were running at full pelt, stumbling and bumping
into each other. 'Dong!' they cried as they ran. 'Dong's
coming!'

Behind them, Dong's roars were getting closer and closer.

'Over here!' Indiana waved his arms. 'Use the bridge.'

'Shaddap, you sap! Dong'll come after them.'

'Don't worry,' Indiana told her. 'When they get across the
bridge we can tip the tree into the ravine so Dong won't be
able to follow.'

Reluctantly Ann nodded. 'I guess so. Come on, come on,'
she called half-heartedly.

Sensing salvation, the crew rushed towards the trunk.

One by one they made their way on to the bridge. Dong crashed through the undergrowth, trees and giant plants splintering in his path.

'He's behind you!' called Indiana, unhelpfully.

The crew hurried on.

Instead of following his prey onto the bridge, Dong reached the edge of the ravine and paused.

'What's he doing?' wondered Ann.

'Maybe he's frightened of heights.'

Ann let out an exasperated sigh. 'He's an ape. They ain't known for sufferin' height phobia, due to them spendin' their lives swinging through the trees.'

'So why isn't he following them?'

Indiana's question was soon answered as Dong reached down and began to lift up the end of the wooden log bridge.

Ann's face was horror-stricken. 'He's going to tip them into the ravine.'

Realizing their predicament, the crew doubled their efforts to cross the bridge before Dong shook them off.

But the beast had other plans for the helpless men. He began to turn the great trunk in his paws, round and round, like a huge rolling pin. The fugitives were forced to stop running along the trunk to safety and instead run on the spot to counteract the rotation, like lumberjacks in a log-rolling competition.

There was a cry as one of the crew lost his footing. He fell, bounced off the spinning tree and was spun into the chasm.

Ann shielded her eyes in horror.

Another crew member failed to keep up with the increasing pace and flew off into the void with a heart-rending scream.

Indiana's face was set grim. 'It's beastly, the way he's playing with them!'

'He's a beast!' pointed out Ann. 'I guess it comes natural.'

Suddenly, Dong stopped spinning the trunk. It came to a juddering halt, catching the remaining crew members unaware. Their momentum sent them staggering forward. Desperately they tried to stop. It was useless. As one, they teetered forwards, backwards then forwards again before flying off the bridge *en masse*, lemming-like. Their screams lasted for several seconds before being cut off. A series of bumps drifted up from the floor of the ravine.

Indiana grimaced. 'Instant pizza.'

'You got a way with a metaphor,' Ann told him.

Across the gulf, Dong held up the tree over his head and

tossed it into the ravine. 'Ruuuuaaaaoooooorrrrr!' His victory cry echoed round the jungle.

Ann tugged at Indiana's sleeve. 'Come on, Bones, let's get outta here before Dong works out a way to get at us.'

Indiana ignored the advice. He stepped up to the edge of the ravine and began taunting the celebrating ape. 'Hey, Dong! You may be big and ugly, but you've got no brains! You just threw away the only thing that could get you over here. How you gonna reach us now, you big monkey!'

Dong pouted aggressively towards Ann and Indiana.

'Yeah, that's right, monkey brains. You're over there but we're over here. You didn't think about that did you, huh?'

'OK, Bones, you've made your point. Let's get outta here.'

But Indiana's testosterone was gushing. He began to ape the ape, leaping about, legs bent and hands hooked under his armpits 'Uw-uw-uw,' he chanted.

Dong glowered.

'Uw-uw-uw.'

Dong began to tramp away from the edge.

'Ha! You monkey chicken. That's it, run away! Uw-uw-uw!'

Dong stopped and turned. He lifted something long and

flexible, and held it out horizontally before him. From a distance it might have been a tree trunk.

'Indiana,' warned Ann. 'He's doing somethin'.'

Indiana was oblivious. 'Uw-uw-uw!'

The ape began to charge towards the ravine.

'Uw-uw … uh?'

'Oh my Gahd, I think he's going to pole-vault!'

Indiana blenched. 'And have you seen what he's using for a pole?'

'I've seen it! I've seen it! Oh my *Gahd* …'

For a moment it looked as though Dong would hurtle over the ravine's edge, but at the last second he slammed his (literal and metaphorical) pole into the ground and vaulted over the gap, landing with an earth-shaking thump next to Indiana and Ann.

'Ruuurrrrr!'

Indiana froze, bow-legged and arms bent. He looked up into the vengeful face of the great beast.

'Uw?'

CHAPTER SIXTEEN

Dong Goes Ape

Ray stood at the entrance to Dong's cave, tapping his foot on the ground. He had completed the finishing touches to his makeover and now awaited Dong's return in a state of nervous excitement.

As the sun sank behind the mountain range, Ray heard the distant thump, thump, thump of giant footfalls. At last! Dong was returning!

Ray gave himself a quick once over in his handy pocket vanity-case mirror and took up a nonchalant pose, leaning against the cave entrance. The giant ape came into view, grunting and groaning.

Ray pointed theatrically at his watch. 'And what time do you call this, Mr Dong? I've been slaving away all day and

you don't even have the decency to call! You could have –'
Ray broke off as he saw what Dong held in his paws:
Indiana and Ann. With each step Dong took, they flopped
around like rag dolls.

'Rooouuurrrr!!'

'Dr Bones!' Ray glanced at Ann, his lips pursed. 'And
look what else the ape's dragged in!'

'Nice to see you too, Ray,' said Ann.

'Ray! You're alive!' cried Indiana.

'Well, obviously. No thanks to you two,' replied Ray,
prissily. 'I could have been ravaged by this dreadful
beast.' He gave a little giggle. 'But there's still plenty of time
for that!'

'Can you get your new best friend to put us down?' said
Ann. 'I feel more tossed about than a Caesar salad.'

'You should be so lucky, dearie.' Ray wagged a finger at
Dong. 'And what do you think you're doing with those
two? You're a big bad Dong! If you don't put them down
right this minute I'm going to have to spank the monkey!'
Ray paused briefly, before breaking into a high-pitched
laugh. 'Ooh I am naughty!'

Dong let out a little moan. 'Orrrreeeeee.'

'I should think so too! Now, hurry up or Ray won't
show Dong his little-wittle surprise just waiting for him.'

'Spare us that, perlease,' said Ann.

Hanging his head, Dong placed his two captives at the entrance to the cave like a cat bringing home a dead sparrow.

Indiana grabbed Ray's arm. 'Ray, you've gotta get out of here. The ape's a psycho. He's just killed most of the rescue party.'

Ray arched an eyebrow. 'I've just spent hours sorting out this cave. I think that's a touch more important than a few dead sailors. There's plenty more seamen in the world.' The dresser gave another high-pitched squeal. 'What *am* I like! Now everyone, come on in and see what Ray's done!'

'But Ray, you don't understand,' protested Indiana. 'We've got to get away from here.'

'All in good time. You just *have* to see my handiwork first!' Ray clapped his hands. 'Showtime! Everyone close your eyes and no peeking!'

'Uurrrroawww!'

'I'll lead the way. Here, let me grab hold of you.'

'Ruuuaaarrr?'

There was a moment's silence that was broken by Ann. 'Have some sense of decency, Ray. Lead the ape by the *hand*.'

Ray humphed. 'Spoilsport! I said no peeking.' Nevertheless, he changed his grip on the ape and led Dong into the cave. Indiana and Ann followed.

'Right! Get ready everyone! And open your eyes after three. One … and a two … and a three!'

Dong opened his eyes. Ray beamed.

The cave had been transformed. The previously dark and cluttered space now had an ethereal quality. Vines and orchids tumbled down the marble-effect walls. Marzipan's crude wall paintings had disappeared, covered by chiffon drapes and a two-tone distressed lilac wash. Whitewashed skulls lined the walls, eyes glowing from the flickering perfumed candles burning inside.

The lake was covered in giant flowering water lilies. Several garden gnomes lined the water's edge.

'I just couldn't resist,' gushed Ray. 'And now for the *pièce de resistance*!' He removed a bamboo screen to reveal a pair of bellows, which he began pumping vigorously with his foot. Streams of water shot up from the middle of the lake. 'It's going to need some heavy pumping to keep the jets going. But I think I know an ape who can!'

Dong just stared at the gushing fountain.

Ray stopped pumping. 'I was looking at a sort of kitsch gothic baroque with a smidgeon of primeval angst. It's so us, Dongie!'

The ape continued to stand transfixed and gruntless.

'You did this?' asked Ann.

Ray beamed. 'All my own handiwork. I'm a bit of an expert at DIY.'

'Yeah, I heard you in the cabin on the voyage,' muttered Ann.

'I'll choose to ignore that remark. So …' Ray flung his arms out wide. 'What do you think?'

Dong's lip began to curl. A deep throaty growl filled the cave. 'Rruuuaarrr!' The ape began to beat at his head.

'Careful, Ray,' warned Indiana. 'I don't think Dong's too impressed with the décor.'

Dong's roars grew louder. Bounding forward with a giant leap, he thrashed at the chiffon drapes, ripping them to pieces. The wall skulls followed, splintering into a thousand shards of bone.

'Somebody's gotten up the wrong side of his cage this morning,' said Ray.

'He's going ape!' screamed Ann.

Indeed he was. The beast's fury at the makeover knew no bounds. The bamboo screens were soon matchsticks; the water lilies became giant frisbees as Dong skimmed them out of the cave. Ann, Indiana and Ray took refuge in a small wall recess.

'You don't like it, do you?' wailed Ray; tears streaming down his face. 'Was it the lilac? I know it's bold. It's a colour you either love or hate!'

Ray's wailing seemed to register in Dong's mind. He beat his chest and let out a blood-curdling roar. Revenge was in his eye as he turned slowly and began advancing on the cowering threesome.

Deadman tugged at a vine hanging down the side of the gate. The great bell on top of the wall rang out.

DING DONG ... DING DONG ... DING DONG ... DING DONG

The huge wooden gates creaked open to reveal a motley collection of pirates and crew, anxiety etched into their faces. Marzipan and Deadman hurried through.

'Better shut them pronto,' advised Deadman. 'Lord knows what might be following.' Several pirates jumped forward and the massive wooden latch was manoeuvred into place.

'Only the two of you?' said a pirate. 'Where're the others?'

Deadman sighed heavily. 'I have some bad news and I want to try and break it gently. Where's the Widow Wendy?'

'Ooooooooooh!' Wendy stepped out from behind a burly pirate and threw her apron over her head.

Deadman grimaced. 'Darnn! Yes, I'm afraid we were ambushed by Dong and a whole bunch of crazy prehistoric creatures. I think it's safe to assume that me and Marzipan are the only survivors. But I do have some good news.'

'What's that?' demanded a quivering pirate.

'I managed to get it all on film!' Deadman brandished the camera. 'It's gonna make me rich.'

Wendy lowered her apron and gave Deadman a lurid wink. 'You and the relict of your fellow executive producer, you mean. Now my poor hubby has gorn to meet his maker, it is incumbent on me, as the wife of his bosom, to look after his business interests. I'm coming to Hollywood with you.'

'Ahh, er ...' Deadman began to back away, clutching the camera to his chest protectively. 'Well you see that's – aarrgghhh!' His foot caught against a protruding rock and he stumbled backwards, letting go of the camera, which shot into the air. Deadman flailed wildly to no avail. The camera arced upwards before falling to the ground. It smashed against a rock and cracked open like a coconut. The film spilled out, unwinding like a toilet roll being chased by a cute Labrador puppy.

Deadman flung himself on the roll of film, trying to protect his precious footage. It was too late. It was ruined. The producer collapsed to the ground, holding his head in his hands. 'Oh, rats!'

Indiana, Ann and Ray had their own problems. Dong lumbered menacingly towards them, blocking off their escape path.

'Grraaoooowwwwww!'

'He's engorged,' moaned Ann.

'You mean enraged,' corrected Indiana.

'I know what I mean, fella.'

'Grraaoooowwwwww!' Dong thumped his mighty chest in an ecstasy of rage.

Ray pouted. 'Everyone's a critic these days.'

Indiana grabbed him by the arm. 'Run, you fool!'

Dong roared again, and lumbered in pursuit as Indiana led Ray and Ann up the stone ramp to a cleft in the cave wall. They squeezed through, and found themselves on a narrow ledge in the mountainside. The wall at their backs trembled with Dong's roars as the infuriated ape tore at the rock in an attempt to widen the cleft and take revenge on his human tormentors.

Ann looked down at the sheer cliff beneath their feet. 'Nice going, Bones. How the hell are we supposed to get off this ledge?'

Looking past her shoulder, Indiana said, in stricken tones, 'Unfortunately, I have a feeling that this will not be a problem.'

'Huh?'

Indiana pointed. Ann screamed.

There was a black blur in the sky and a thunder of beating wings as a huge reptilian, bird-like creature swooped down upon them.

'It's a pterodactyl!' cried Indiana.

Ray gave a squeak of alarm. 'It's going to bite us!'

'They can't bite,' said Indiana. 'Pterodactyls have no teeth. They swallow their prey whole.'

'Oh well, that's a comfort.'

The pterodactyl clasped Indiana in its right talon and Ray in its left.

Indiana glared at Ann. 'Do something!'

'Like what?' demanded Ann. A thought struck her. 'Hey – is that thing male?'

Indiana cast a frightened glance at the pterosaur's pendulous undercarriage. 'I think so.'

'Then maybe I do have an idea.' Ann slid between the pterodactyl's captives, reached up, and grabbed two handfuls of the creature's reproductive organs. The pterodactyl froze in mid-flap and made a noise that sounded suspiciously like, 'Ulp!'

'OK, Terry Dactil or whatever your stupid name is, have I got your attention?'

The pterodactyl nodded frantically.

'Good. Now, you're our ticket out of here. You're flying us back to the village and I'm the pilot. When I squeeze left, we go left, I squeeze right, we go right. I squeeze with both hands and you fly like you're gonna lose something very important, which if you don't is in fact the case. Follow my drift?'

The creature nodded again. Behind it, Dong began to lever his massive body through the widening cleft.

'Chocks away!' Ann squeezed both hands tightly. The pterodactyl took off like a chicken with a boot up the backside.

'That's the way to do it, Bones,' she called out. 'The universal male language. Luckily for us, I speak it fluently!'

Dong heaved himself onto the ledge and grabbed – but

too late. The pterodactyl flew off into the setting sun, leaving Dong standing on the mountainside beating his chest and roaring.

Back in the village, Deadman was still inconsolable. 'My movie, ruined. I'm ruined.'

Nevertheless, he was roused from his misery by the flapping of mighty wings, and looked up just as a giant flying reptile landed in the village square with its uninvited passengers. The creature's face looked drained. It opened its claws, releasing Ray and Indiana, who staggered clear, trembling in every limb.

Ann let go of the 'controls'. 'Thanks,' she said. 'I enjoyed my flight, and I hope I'll be travelling with you again real soon.'

The creature gave its great head a decisive shake, uttered a high-pitched squawk, and flew off.

The pirates and remaining crew gathered round as Ann and Indiana, interrupting and contradicting each other every few seconds, related the story of their escape. Deadman grew even more disconsolate. 'I'm sorry I wasn't there with you,' he mumbled.

'You should be, you putz,' snapped Ann. 'Abandoning us like that.'

'If I'd been there I could have captured it all on film.' Oblivious to Ann's scowl, Deadman shook his head in despair. Then he looked up as inspiration struck. 'That's it! How stupid am I? It's not the movie that people will pay to see – it's the star!' Deadman was suddenly transformed, reinvigorated by the vision of dollar signs lighting up before his eyes. 'Dong's worth more than all the movies in the whole wide world!'

'You're not getting me back in that jungle!' warned Ann.

Wendy nodded. 'And my lot ain't going to be keen, either.'

'We won't have to go chasing after Dong,' replied Deadman. 'We've got something he wants.'

All eyes turned to Marzipan, who sat in the sand guzzling Kava from a coconut shell.

Marzipan shook his head. 'Marzipan not wanted by Dong any more. Marzipan should never have become partner of Dong. Marzipan make big cock-up with Dong.'

'You said it, honey,' remarked Ann.

'I'm not talking about jungle boy,' said Deadman. 'I mean Ray.'

The dresser, who had remained strangely silent since the rescue, put a hand to his chest. 'Me? You think Dong wants me? Really? But do you think he'll forgive me?'

'Of course,' said Deadman. 'It's just a tiff – he'll get used to your little ways.'

'But how do you plan to get us back together again?'

DONG … DONG … DONG …

Ray was cut off by the sound of the alarm bell and the panic-stricken cries of the pirates manning the wall, beyond which Dong's roars cut through the jungle night. They were distinct and purposeful. 'Raaaayyyy! Raaaaayyy!'

Deadman grinned. 'Does that answer your question?'

Ray fanned his face with his hand. 'Oh my, I'm going to be ravished! Where's my make-up?'

'Don't worry,' said Wendy. 'The wall will keep him back … I think.'

There was a mighty thumping at the gate. The great wooden structure began to splinter.

Marzipan shuddered. 'It suddenly occur to Marzipan that including gates that Dong can comfortably walk through in impregnable stone wall might be considered a bit of a design flaw.'

Pirates and crew hurried to the creaking gates in a frantic effort to hold Dong back. Desperately they crowded against the wooden structure. Their efforts were futile. With a mighty crack, the wooden latch cracked in two, the bolts and chains flew in all directions and the gates were flung open.

Dong beat his chest and roared. All the human inhabitants of Skullandcrossbones Island were at the beast's mercy.

CHAPTER SEVENTEEN

Sing Alonga Dong

'Roooooaaaaaaaaarrrrrrrrr!'

Deadman stared up at Dong. 'Oh, boy. Does he look pissed!'

Wendy hid her face in her apron. 'We're doomed! Doomed!'

'Don't worry.' A manic grin spread over Deadman's face. 'I have a plan for this contingency.' The maverick director grabbed his costume designer by the sleeve and hustled him away. 'Ray, I need you for this.'

Dong spent a few moments reducing the gates to matchwood before descending on the village like an Old Testament prophet with a mission to smite the heathen. The giant ape ignored the feeble resistance of the remaining pirates, and the imprecations of Ann who, heedless of personal danger, was following him around, screaming insults and swiping ineffectually at his giant hairy ankles. Enraged beyond endurance by Ray's perfidy and stylistic excesses, Dong rampaged through the village like an elephant with a sore butt, demolishing bamboo huts (and their occupants) and bellowing defiance.

The unfinished theme park built in his honour seemed to arouse Dong to even greater extremes of ire. Screaming islanders dodged ballistic dodgem cars as Dong tore up the track. Before long the ghost train gave up the ghost and the Fun House became a fun demolition site. Helter-skelters were hurled hither and thither. The bamboo Ferris wheel went spinning over the wall like an oversized discus. The swingboats were sunk, the roller-coaster was toast, the roundabouts were down and out and the Hall of Mirrors smashed beyond repair. Huddled behind the counter of a hoop-la stall, Indiana pulled his hat over his ears and waited for the end.

Ray had managed to gather Marzipan and five survivors from the village and was now rummaging feverishly in his costume boxes.

'Marzipan don't see why he should help lousy chiseller

who stole Dong from him,' grumbled Marzipan. 'What Ray looking for anyway?'

'Costumes, Mr Thicky!' Ray ground his teeth. 'And you should help because this whole situation is all your fault and Dong is going to trash the whole village and everyone in it unless we do something. Mr Deadman's got a plan. Oh, where are those "Cage aux Folles" costumes?' He threw up his hands. 'Honestly, I've only got to turn my back for five minutes and everything's higgledy-piggledy. Oh well, we'll have to make do with what we've got. Let's see now: a motorcycle cop, a sailor, a cowboy, an American Indian, a leather fetishist and a hard-hat construction worker … yes …' said Ray slowly, a creative gleam sparking in his eyes, 'yes, we can do something with this.'

Down on the beach, Deadman was bellowing out directions.

'Put those rifles down, men,' he ordered his nervous guards. 'They're no use against Dong anyhow! What we need is right there in those crates! Break them open!'

The guards set to with a will. 'What's in the crates, Mr Deadman?' demanded the petty officer in charge of the party eagerly. 'Grenades? Gas bombs? Land mines? Flame-throwers?'

'None of the above.' Deadman's grin would have got him sectioned under the Mental Health Act in any civilized community. 'Open 'em up, you'll see.'

After a deal of heaving and grunting, the lid came off the first crate. The eager guards grabbed at the contents – and withdrew their hands clutching small brown paper packages with stencilled labels.

'"Yun Chow House of Heavenly Rapture",' read the officer. '"Exporting mind-altering substances since 1828".' He held out the package with a bewildered expression. 'What's this?'

'Opium,' said Deadman succinctly. 'High grade. A ton and a half of it.'

'And what are we supposed to do with a ton and a half of high-grade opium?'

By way of reply, Deadman licked his finger and held it up 'Yup, wind's in the right direction.' He gave another manic grin. 'We're gonna burn it.'

Deadman gave the guards further directions, then sprinted back to the village. He arrived during a momentary lull in the destruction. Dong had discovered the Test Your Strength machine and was amusing himself by tapping the striker with his little finger and making the bell ring every time. Ann had apparently given up attacking

Dong. Noticing Deadman, she slouched over to him. Indiana broke cover and joined them.

'So what now?' Ann demanded.

'Mr Deadman! Over here!'

Deadman looked around, and spotted Ray's beckoning finger. He winked at Ann and Indiana. 'It's all under control. You're about to watch a real operator at work. Learn from the professionals, kids.' Deadman led Ann and Indiana between wrecked rides and stalls to join Ray and his party.

Ann stared at Marzipan and his strangely garbed companions. 'What's this, trick or treat?'

Ray smoothed down his leather blouson. 'These are all the costumes I could find,' he said defensively. 'Don't worry, Mr Deadman, it'll work.'

Indiana gave a mirthless laugh. 'Whatever this plan is, I'll believe that when I see it.'

The Lord of the Jungle evidently shared their misgivings. He fingered his hard hat with disapproval. 'Marzipan feel like a pillock.'

Deadman sniffed the air. 'Oh, well – show time. Here comes the smoke.' He patted Ray on the shoulder. 'Give it a little time to build, then you're on.'

The movie man was right. Down on the beach, a ton and

a half of best-quality opium (tended by members of the *Vulture*'s crew who had suddenly become very keen on their work, though they were also suddenly a trifle ham-fisted and inclined to giggle for no obvious reason) was smouldering nicely.

Across the clearing, Dong's head jerked up as the fumes from the fire reached him. Nostrils the size of air conditioning ducts widened. Dong took a great lungful of the fragrant smoke, and slowly a dazed, beatific smile crossed the giant ape's face. Dong inhaled again …

Ray bit his lip. 'You sure this will work?'

'It never fails in Hollywood.' Deadman tapped Ray on the shoulder. 'On my mark!'

The movie director stepped from cover and marched up to Dong. 'Hey, there! Handsome!'

Dong gave an interrogative grunt and looked blearily around. Seeing no other creature to whom Deadman's remarks could possibly have been addressed, the gigantic ape raised his sofa-sized eyebrows and hesitantly lifted a hairy finger to point at his own chest.

'Yes, I mean you! Hold it right there!' Deadman prowled around Dong, making a camera frame from his thumbs and index fingers. 'Yeah … yeah … yeah. Tell me, kid,' he breezed, 'did anyone ever tell you you should be in the movies?'

Dong gave his head a bewildered shake. Something at the back of his mind was hammering on the door of his consciousness, which seemed to have become unexpectedly wedged shut. A small, insistent voice was reminding him that he should be squashing Deadman like a bug. But somehow ... Dong inhaled again. He let out a grunt that sounded very like, 'Ohhhhh, wwowwww!'

'Yessir,' Deadman continued in a voice that was only slightly muffled by the handkerchief he held over the lower part of his face, 'you're an ape in a million. You just reek of star quality. You're wasted on this island – hanging with a bunch of low-life pirates, kibitzing with dinosaurs who haven't even got the initiative to evolve – you're just a big fish in a small pond, Dong baby! You need to be where it's at, where it's all happening. Don't be afraid to dream! You got what it takes! Trust me, kid, and your name will be in lights! Hit it, Ray!'

A fortuitous moonbeam struck Deadman as he made this announcement. Dong roared approval. In the background, the sound of waves crashing on to the beach juxtaposed with the cries of sea birds. Three distinct strident chords broke through the night air to be quickly replaced by a thin tune.

215

Drums cut in, beating a thudding rhythm. The music swelled and the dazzled Dong watched entranced as Deadman made way for a group of six figures who pranced into view and launched into an outrageously camp dance routine. Their voices echoed around the remains of Dongland:

'*Come out, come out, come out, come out!*' they chorused.

Stamping their feet, twirling and gyrating, Marzipan and his troupe strutted their funky stuff.

'*Whatever,*' they chorused.

Ray took the solo line:

'*Let's go far away:*

(Whatever) We can leave today

(Whatever) Put yourself in our hands

(Whatever) We can take you to the promised land

(Whatever) We can reach the sky

(Whatever) Kiss your ape goodbye

(Whatever) You will go so far

(Whatever) You're gonna be a star!'

Dong clapped his hands and roared with approval as the dancers launched into the chorus:

'*(Come West) Come to Hollywood*

(Come West) Where the air is good

(Come West) Where they love showbiz

216

(Come West) Where the money is ...'

All over the battered remains of their township, pirates and sailors from the *Vulture*'s crew emerged from their places of refuge to bolster the effort that seemed to be achieving the impossible: rendering their giant nemesis compliant and harmless. The pirates danced a hornpipe, the sailors did a hand-jive.

'(Whatever) You'll live like a king
(Whatever) You'll have everything
(Whatever) Self-indulgence is
(Whatever) A way of life in Los Angeles
(We want you) Put your name on the line
(We want you) Hell, don't read it, just sign
(This contract) Is binding legally
(For how long?) For eternity!'

Pan and the Lost Boys appeared, contributing pogo, dead fly and breakdance moves to the party. Tiger Lilly and her Indians (who had noticed that an apparent member of their ethnic group was already involved in the routine) emerged from the jungle to add a war-dance to the proceedings.

'(Come West) Come to Hollywood
(Come West) Where the air is good
(Come West) Dongie, come and see
(Come West) We'll live in luxury (Arrr!)

(Come West) Where there's golden sand
(Come West) Where the life is grand
(Come West) Where they love showbiz
(Come West) Where the money is.

There where the sky is blue
You can screw (Screw)
Who you want to screw (Ooh Arr Ooh Arr!)
And if there should be a fuss (Arr!)
The cops (You'll find) Will always side with us (Arr!)'

Dinosaurs had now begun to emerge from the jungle. T
Rex was jiving with the iguanadon. A double line of
velociraptors swung into the Gay Gordons. A rhythm
section of stegosaurii rattled their great back-vanes and
stamped, creating a percussive beat. Apatosaurus and
diplodocus swayed from side to side, underpinning the
chorus with a deep, throbbing bass as a squadron of
pteradons performed a formation fly-past. Marzipan and
his sweating, posturing troupe swung into the final verse of
their number:

'*(You'll find that) There are drugs galore*
(Moreover) Bunnies by the score!
(Don't worry) It's easy to acquire
(On Sunset) Every craving that your heart desires!

(In L.A.) It's easy to get boned
(In L.A.) You'll spend your whole life stoned
(If your face) Lacks personality
(We'll cure that) With Rhinoplasty.

(Come West) Come to Hollywood
(Come West) Where the air is good
(Come West) Where they love showbiz
(Come West) Where the money is
(Come West) Come to Hollywood
(Come West) Where the air is good
(Come West) Dongie, come and see
(Come West) We'll live in luxury (Arrr!)
Come on, come on, come on, come on
(Come West) Where you can set the trend
(Come West) Where you can sue your friends
(Come West) Where they love showbiz
(Come West) Where the money is
(Come on, come on, come on) ...'

Bedazzled by the music, bewildered by the potent fumes of opium, Dong swayed, eyes glazed. Deadman stepped forward with a magnum of champagne whose contents he tipped into an ice bucket, which he offered to the befuddled primate. He followed up this gesture by thrusting a contract into Dong's left hand and a pen into his right.

'Trust me, Dong baby!' he yelled. 'You're gonna be a celebrity – no, don't eat the pen! I'll get you out of this jungle! I'll put your name in lights coast to coast. I'll even make you an executive producer! Sign here.'

Squinting, the zonked ape made an X on the paper.

As Indiana boggled and Ann glowered, Deadman held the precious contract aloft. 'Yes! Prepare to refloat the ship, men! We're going home – and we're taking Dong with us!'

'You're crazy!' Indiana grabbed the ecstatic movie-maker by the shoulders. 'No chains will hold that beast.'

Deadman brandished the contract in Indiana's face. 'This contract will bind him tighter than any chains ever made. We're millionaires, men! Think of the headlines: "Dong, the Eighth Wonder of the World." He patted the swaying Dong with proprietorial affection. 'Trust me, kid. This is your big break. I'm gonna make you a STAR!'

CHAPTER EIGHTEEN

Dong Flops

It was three years before Indiana returned to the United States and found himself in Los Angeles.

Broken-hearted by Ann's continuing rejection of his advances, he had left the *Vulture* when the ship called at Cape Town on the way back from Skullandcrossbones island. After that, his calling had taken him to the farthest corners of the Earth. His expedition to find the Green Eye of the Little Yellow God had proved to be a disappointment. A rival explorer, Mad Carew, had beaten him to it by a matter of three weeks. However, he had taken some comfort from the news that Mad Carew had shortly thereafter been found pinned to the wall with an oriental dagger (presumably inserted between the third and fourth ribs by the worshippers of the Little Yellow God, who seemed to have a negative attitude towards acquisitive archaeology).

Indiana had by this time become involved in a spot of bother involving the Ark of the Convent (which had led to an unpleasant misunderstanding with the Little Sisters of Saint Assumpta, who had only with difficulty been persuaded not to press charges). He had followed this up with a rather fraught visit to the Temple of Gloom, where his misadventures had set mineral extraction in Uttar Pradesh back by several decades. Finally, there had been the affair of the Holy Flail (at least, that was how Indiana described the particular archaeological relic with which he had been discovered, naked except for a blindfold, in a motel room in the company of a lady wearing a rubber basque, who gave her name as Mme Fifi la Touche).

All in all, it had been an incident-packed thirty-six months, and Indiana had been thankful to return to the States for a rest, and to await the elapse of statutes of limitations in various countries whose authorities he had recently upset. So he was feeling somewhat jaded as he wandered into a bar on Sunset Boulevard and ordered a Bloody Mary. He had just taken a seat and raised the glass to his lips when a familiarly ear-grating voice from a neighbouring booth made him prick up his ears.

'Don't tell me I gotta "keep up appearances", Deadman, you lousy four-flusher. Everyone in this town knows my marriage has hit more rocks than the Hoover Dam Construction Company.'

Indiana scrambled to the end of the bench seat and peered round the divider separating his booth from its neighbour. 'Ann? Deadman?'

Ann looked up briefly. 'Oh boy. The bad dime's back.' She turned her attention back to her cocktail.

'Dr Bones!' Deadman was more cordial than his companion, but he looked strained. He had put on weight and had the unkempt air of one who has no pressing need to ensure that he looks his best on getting up in the morning. 'What brings you to LA?'

Ignoring Ann's less-than-welcoming glance, Indiana slid into the booth beside Deadman. 'Just passing. I thought I'd call around and see how you're all doing. And Dong, of course.'

Ann said, 'Ha!' A spasm of pain flitted across Deadman's face.

'That good, eh?' Indiana gave Ann a sympathetic look from which a trace of *schadenfreude* was not entirely absent. 'I couldn't help overhearing – I gather you're married, but it isn't going so well. Who's the ungrateful slob?'

Ann puckered up as though she were sucking lemons. With every appearance of reluctance at having to sully her lips with the monosyllable, she answered, 'Dong.'

Indiana gaped at her. 'But isn't he …? I mean, aren't you …?'

'If you're trying, in your inarticulate way, to ask me why I married a thirty-foot ape who wouldn't know what to do with a woman if she came with an instruction manual, the answer is, "Beats the hell outta me".' Ann downed the remainder of her cocktail and stood up. 'Thanks for the drink, Deadman. You'll be hearing from my attorney.'

With this parting shot, Ann stalked out of the bar. Deadman sighed, and knocked back his bourbon.

Indiana indicated his empty glass. 'What'll you have?'

'Bourbon. With a bourbon chaser.' As Indiana signalled the waiter, Deadman said, 'That's all I need.'

'But what's with this marriage?' Indiana was nonplussed. 'I thought Dong and Ann hated each other.'

'Sure they do. Always have.' Deadman took a pull from his refreshed glass. 'What's that got to do with anything?'

'But why did they get married, if …?'

Dong Flops

'Pretty green, aren't you?' Deadman gave Indiana a conspiratorial wink. 'It was a marriage of convenience. She's his beard. Happens all the time in Hollywood. See, when the public go to see a movie, the men expect the hero to be more macho than a Mexican steelworker, and the women – God bless 'em – like to imagine him making love to them. Nobody wants to have it brought to their attention that the guy's actually as gay as a revivalist picnic. So actors in that position get married as a kind of smokescreen. It doesn't mean they're married in the biblical sense. Dong's still with Ray.' Deadman's face clouded. 'Leastways, last I heard. The two of them have been fighting like cat and dog lately.'

Indiana shook his head in resignation. 'I guess I'll never get used to Hollywood ways. Anyhow – I've been out of the country for the past three years. How did Dong do when you got him over here?'

Deadman rolled his glass between his palms for a full half-minute before replying. Then he said, 'Well, after you jumped ship – good decision, by the way: the trip back across the Atlantic was a nightmare. I mean, it was bad enough cleaning up Dong's dung, but when he started to get seasick …

'Anyway, to begin with he was a sensation! We shot the

225

movie on the back lot in three weeks – but then it took us six months in post-production to figure out how Dong could have a convincing battle with a guy in a rubber T Rex suit. Then there were problems with the title. The front office insisted on calling the movie *King Dong*. I thought that was kind of silly because Dong never was a king and I couldn't see anything wrong with my title, but go figure studio executives. Anyway, the movie was a smash, and after that I did a deal with United, and they teamed Dong with Marzipan for a couple of sequels.

'After that, things started to go downhill. The critics loved Dong to begin with but by the third movie they were staring to bitch about "same old, same old", and anyway Marzipan got tired of second billing and split to star in jungle flicks.

'Well, we needed another success by then. Dong wanted to increase his range, so he'd be taken seriously as an actor: he didn't want to be known only for monster movies. So I tried to find him a role in light comedy. He tested for *Bringing up Baby* with Hepburn and Grant, but that idiot Hawks insisted on casting a leopard – can you imagine? A leopard!'

'Tough luck.'

'Yeah. So I gave him a run out in heart-warming family

226

drama – but Capra, damn his eyes, insisted on cutting his part in *It's a Wonderful Life*. Apparently Jimmy Stewart complained that the scene where George Bailey hired Dong to rub out Old Man Potter didn't fit in with his image. I mean, give me a break!'

Indiana nodded sympathetically.

'So then we cast him as an action hero in *Dong Air* and *Judge Dong*. No good. He couldn't master the dialogue.'

'I thought the dialogue in action movies was mostly grunts?'

'It is, but he still couldn't handle it. I'd invested too much in his career by then to give up, so we wrote a couple of movies around him, but *Dongle All the Way* was a disaster, and *Kindergarten Dong* wasn't much better. He even had a go at erotic movies – *Last Dongo in Paris*. We got through four hundred pounds of butter and half a dozen leading ladies before we eventually had to pull the picture. Then we tried him in musicals.'

'Oh, brother.'

'Tell me about it. *Chitty Chitty Dong Dong, The Dong and I, Hello Dongy!* Stinkers, the lot of them.'

'I didn't even know Dong could sing.'

'He can't. We dubbed him. That wasn't the problem. Have you ever seen a thirty-foot ape try to tap-dance? It's pathetic. Then at last he had a success – playing Quasimodo in *The Hunchback of Notre Dong*. Things looked rosy for a while, but then along came another calamity – *The Dongfather*. Nobody could understand a word he said in that movie.

'That's when he started hitting the banana juice big time. Before long he was a thirty-bottle-a-day ape. So we admitted defeat and decided he ought to go back to what he was good at, you know? We put him in a low-budget monster movie – *King Dong Versus Zorilla*.'

'That sounds a sure-fire smash!'

'Sure – until you realize that a zorilla is a skunk-like mammal from Africa, only slightly bigger than a weasel. With the finance we were getting at that point, it was all we could afford. It wasn't much of a contest, to be brutally honest. The movie went down the toilet along with Dong's career. These days he can't even get a job doing voice-overs for Disney.'

'It sounds like you've tried everything.'

'That's the conclusion I came to.' Deadman finished his drink. 'I finally wised up. I realized what had been staring me in the face all along. Dong is only good for one type of role. That's why for his comeback picture I'm going into production with the biggest creature feature ever.'

'I guess that makes sense,' said Indiana.

'It can't fail! We've got an all-star cast. Dong's going up against every monster in the history of the movies – Godzilla, Mothra, the Beast from 20,000 Fathoms, The Thing, It, Them, the Fifty-Foot Woman, the Creature from the Black Lagoon, the Monster from the Id, the Invisible Man (if we can ever find the schmuck), the Blob, the Hulk, Shelob, the Nazgul, Dracula, Frankenstein, the Wolfman, the Mummy, the Killer Tomatoes, the Daleks and those things from *Tremors*, I don't know what they're called but boy are they scary!' Deadman picked up his fedora. 'I'm off to see Dong right now. Why not come along?'

Indiana shrugged. He had nothing better to do. He paid the tab and followed Deadman out of the door.

As they neared Don's domicile, the neighbourhood gave Indiana a fair indication of the depth of Dong's failure. This sure wasn't Beverley Hills. Peeling apartment blocks and squalid condos lined streets strewn with garbage and cars that had been Last Year's Model in 1926.

Deadman stopped the cab at a grey house. He led Indiana through a grey gate into a grey yard. There, lounging listlessly beside an empty swimming pool, was Dong.

Indiana was shocked to see the change that had come

229

over the terror of Skullandcrossbones Island. Dong was overweight, even for a thirty-foot gorilla, and his fur was turning grey and coming out in handfuls. He wore cracked designer sunglasses, presumably made to measure in his glory days. He also wore Bermuda shorts, a soiled Hawaiian shirt that would have been sufficiently revolting on a human being of normal proportions but on Dong's gargantuan body was offensive on an epic scale, and an ice pack.

Deadman cast a jaundiced eye on the litter of empty bottles that covered the bottom of the pool. 'Hey, Dong! I brought an old friend to see you.'

'Gwooooaaaarrrr?'

'Indiana Bones – Skullandcrossbones Island, remember?'

'Wrrrrrrrrrrrr?'

'No, just visiting. He just dropped by to see how you were doing.'

'Grrrooooaaaaarrrrr.' Dong took a swig from his bottle.

'Yeah, I guess that's pretty obvious. Hey, listen, Dong baby, about Ann: it's not good news. She won't listen to reason. She wants the car, the beach house and seventy per cent of your other assets, such as they are.'

'Rrrrroaaaarrrrgggghh.' Dong lit a cigar and coughed alarmingly.

'I told her that but she won't buy it. Listen, don't worry. The new movie will make you a fortune, and she's already dumped you, so she won't ever see a cent of it. You and Ray will have enough to start again and –'

'Urrggehhhoouuurrr!'

'Who's a no-good scheming little weasel?' Deadman paled. 'Uh-oh. Don't tell me you and Ray have had another fight?'

In response, Dong held his head in his hands and rocked.

'I swear, you guys are such a pair of –' Deadman broke off as the poolside phone rang. 'I'll get it.' He picked up the receiver, listened for a moment, then passed it to Dong. 'It's for you. It's Ray.'

Dong picked up the phone delicately between an enormous thumb and forefinger, as a human being might handle a caterpillar, and held it to his ear. 'Grrrrr?'

The phone squawked.

'Grrroooooaaaa?'

The phone squawked again.

'Rrrrrrrrrooooooooooooaaaaaaaaaaaaaaawwwwwwwgggggggh hhhhhhhhh!'

The phone clicked as the line went dead. Staring at nothing, Dong let the receiver slip from his fingers to clatter among the empty bottles at the bottom of the pool.

King Dong

Deadman turned an appalled face to Indiana. 'Dong says Ray's leaving him!'

CHAPTER NINETEEN

So Long, Dong

The Great Director was haranguing his crew:

'All right, men, we're about to shoot the most expensive scene in Hollywood history. When I give the word, we set fire to the city walls. Planes will drop incendiaries. When the guys up in the hills see the smoke, they release millions of gallons of water, which will sweep two thousand extras away in a devastating flood – they don't know what's coming so we'll get some genuine reactions. The set for Sodom and Gomorrah and all the costumes have cost us millions and they're going to be destroyed in an instant. We can only afford to do this once, so I don't want any mistakes. Everybody clear? OK, let's do it.'

A few minutes later the director cried, 'Action!'

The walls of Sodom and Gomorrah burned. Flame fell from the sky. A rumbling announced the arrival of the flood. The extras turned, screaming in unfeigned horror, to face the wall of water that would sweep all away.

And a thirty-foot ape wandered into the middle of the shot and bellowed, 'Raaaaaaaaayyyyyyyyyyyyyyy!'

The Great Director tore his hair. 'Cut! Cut!' He turned in mute appeal to the operator of the principal camera, who shook his head.

But there was still a chance – if the second camera, up on the hills, had captured the action from a different angle, maybe they could stitch the scene together, save something from the wreck.

The Great Director raised his megaphone and bellowed, 'Hey! You up there! Did you get it? Did you get it?'

The operator of the second camera waved his hat cheerfully. His distant cry echoed round the lot like the voice of doom:

'Ready when you are, Mr de Mille!'

Deadman turned beseechingly to Indiana. 'Did you see where he went?'

Indiana shook his head.

'He's going crazy – trying to find Ray. He'll trash the

whole town if he doesn't. Listen, Ray's on the evening flight to New York. I'll take a cab to the airport and head him off. You go get Ann.'

Indiana stared. 'What can she do?'

'She's his wife, goddammit, she's got to be able to do something! Get going!'

The bearded astronaut slipped from his horse and knelt before the remains of the Statue of Liberty, beating upon the unresisting sand with clenched fists. 'You maniacs!' he howled. 'You blew it up! Damn you! Damn you all to hell!'

'Raaaaaaaaayyyyyyyyyyyyyyyy!' A giant ape ploughed through the statue as though it wasn't there, reducing it to rubble. The bearded man stared at its retreating figure.

'On the other hand,' he said, 'maybe apes took over the world because they just grew so damn *big*.'

At the Panoramic lot, on Sound Stage 3, the cameras rolled as a much-damaged robot with burning red eyes menaced a young woman who had clearly not been having a fun time recently.

'You are finished, woman of the paast,' ranted the mechanical monster. 'I haave been shot aat, hit by speeding trucks, blown up, and steeel I follow you. The evil robot geniuses who built me designed my body to be invulnerable to all threats.'

A gigantic hairy foot smashed through the roof of the stage and crushed the robot into scrap. Cogwheels flew all over the place. From somewhere far above came a distant howl of, 'Raaaaaaaaayyyyyyyyyyyyyyyy!'

As the perplexed crew exchanged glances, the robot – now looking as if it had been in an argument with a car crusher – concluded: 'All threats except thaat of being stamped on by a thirty-foot gorilla. Hasta la vista, baby.'

The robot exploded. Terminally.

On the back lot a worried director was quizzing his production manager. 'You sure those guns are loaded with blanks?'

The production manager nodded wearily.

'OK, then, here we go. Action!'

The clapperboard clicked. '*Gunfight at the OK Corral*, scene thirty-six, take one.'

'Action!'

The Earps and Doc Holliday eyed the Clantons and their allies, hands hovering over their guns, alert as snakes. The stand-off was about to end in violence and tragedy.

There was a thunder of pounding feet, and a great

rushing wind. The dust of the corral was blown up into choking clouds, which reduced visibility to zero. From the eye of the tornado came a despairing bellow:

'Raaaaaaaaayyyyyyyyyyyy!'

When the dust cleared, the Earps, the Clantons and their sidekicks were scattered around like broken dolls, lolling against walls, hanging over fences.

The director turned an ashen face to his production manager. 'Are you *sure* you put blanks in those guns?'

Over at Paranoid, a teen movie was shooting on Sound Stage One:

'Gee, this fraternity party is cool.'

'Don't you feel the atmosphere is kinda electric with unresolved tensions?'

'Yeah, remember that guy we ran over last summer, and we burned his body and dumped it in the lake?'

'Carley, we swore we'd never ever talk about the guy we ran over last summer, whose body we burned and dumped in the lake.'

'Leave me alone, Sidney. You're just jealous because I got to be Prom Queen instead of you.'

The roof of the set peeled back like the lid of a sardine can. A giant hairy hand appeared and began picking up co-eds, one by one. Giant bloodshot eyeballs examined each in turn; as every squealing starlet proved not to be the object of his search, Dong bellowed, 'Raaaaaaaaayyyyyyyyyyyyyyy!' and hurled her aside.

Off camera, a character in a black cloak and a distorted white mask sat back, lit a cigarette, put his feet up, and reached for a magazine. 'Me, they don't need.'

The hard-eyed cop stood over his rat-like quarry in a firing stance.

'This here's a .44 Magnum,' he rasped through clenched teeth, 'the most powerful and phallically symbolic handgun in the world, and I'm a borderline psychopath masquerading as a public servant. Now, you're probably askin' yourself whether I just fired six shots or only five. To tell you the truth, I kinda lost count myself. So you'll just have to ask yourself one question: Do I feel lucky? Well, do ya, punk?'

His snivelling victim suddenly brightened. 'Yeah.'

'Is that so?' The cop's eyes narrowed to slits. 'Why?'

'Because there's a thirty-foot ape comin' up behind you, and he's about to stomp you into a little splash of shit.'

The actor playing the cop looked bemused. 'You sure that's your line?'

His victim gave a manic grin. 'It is now …'

Amid the shocking violence of a special-effects battle, a small oasis of calm had formed around the tired-looking captain and the bedraggled soldier.

'Private,' said the captain, 'I dragged my men through hell and high water to find you. All your brothers done got themselves killed, but Uncle Sam, God bless him, has sent me across half of Europe to bring you back to your maw and paw. We seen war in all its ugliness, we seen things that no man ever should see. A lot of us didn't make it. But we're here to save you, Private Brian. You're comin' with us. You're goin' home.'

A giant foot descended like the wrath of God. STOMP!

'Raaaaaaaaayyyyyyyyyyyyyyyy!'

The captain stood over the remains of Private Brian and rubbed his eyes. 'Oh, perfect!'

The slack-jawed man with the military haircut stared at the package of confectionery that lay in his lap. 'Mah momma used ter say,' he drawled, 'life is like a box of chocolates, you never know what you're gonna git …'

Dong stampeded across the shot. 'Raaaaaaaaaa-yyyyyyyyyyyyyy!'

'… though I do declare,' the half-wit admitted, 'I wasn't expecting that.'

'Ann!' Indiana waved his arms. 'Dong's on the rampage – you gotta calm him down!'

'Hah!' Ann glowered. 'What makes you think I can calm the big lug down?'

'You're his wife – can't you threaten to make him sleep on the couch or something?'

'We're getting divorced, in case you'd forgotten.'

Inspiration struck Indiana. 'Well, how's he gonna pay you alimony if every studio in town is suing him for damages?'

Ann stood up with sudden decision. 'You're right – we gotta stop the big ape before somebody gets hurt.'

The Emperor raged at his victim.

'Renegade!' he cried. 'Traitor to the great Empire of Rome. Prepare to meet your death on the blood-soaked sands of the arena!'

The gladiator faced his accuser, head held high. 'My name is Maximus Garrulus Hellraisus, father of a murdered wife, husband of a murdered son … or the other way about, whatever, I had a few beers last night, you can edit that bit … Anyway, my name is Maximus Garrulus Hellraisus, and I am afraid of nothing in this world!'

The Colosseum rocked as Dong pounded through, squashing a couple of lions, a leopard and a rhinoceros on the way.

The gladiator felt the fear trickling down his hairy legs. 'With the possible exception of that.'

The bearded New Zealander gazed lovingly at the set.

His designer permitted himself a smile of satisfaction. 'It's finished, Mr J. It's perfect – a complete recreation of a block in the Big Apple, right here in Hollywood, just like you wanted. Correct in every detail, right down to the lettering on the billboards. At last we're ready to shoot the crowd scenes.'

Dong tore through the immaculately realized set like a fleet of bulldozers. 'Raaaaaaaaayyyyyyyyyyyyyyyy!'

The designer stared at the ruins. 'Didn't you tell me the scenes where he trashes New York would be model shots?'

The director raised clenched fists to the heavens and cried, 'Who let that bloody ape in here?'

Deadman turned away from the check-in desk and

swore. He was too late – Ray's plane had already boarded.

He tore out of the terminal building, and screeched to a halt on hearing a squawking voice from a police car parked next to the kerb delivering a frantic APB: 'Calling all cars ... calling all cars ... Dong is heading for the Hollywood Hills.'

Deadman hailed a cab and dived into the back seat. 'Follow that thirty-foot gorilla!'

Flames were rising all over Tinseltown as Dong climbed the hills overlooking the city. The great ape was driven by a vague idea that if he could get to some high vantage point he might be able to spot his lost love. Breathing hard, because he hadn't kept in shape the last couple of years, the huge beast laboriously climbed to the top of the great white HOLLYWOOD sign that loomed over the valley.

A droning sound met his ears. Dong roared defiance at a flight of biplanes, returning to base from shooting a WW1 dogfight for *The Red Baron*. The startled pilots, finding their flight path unexpectedly obstructed, banked away in panic, but not before two of their number had been swatted out of the sky by the frantic ape.

'Raaaaaaaaaayyyyyyyyyyyyyyyy!'

A few miles away, on the flight deck of an experimental rocket ship, a heavily muscled football player was wrestling with a wide-eyed, bearded maniac. 'You're insane, Jerkov!' roared the testosterone-charged superman. 'There's no such person as Ping the Merciless, there's no such place as Planet Pungo, and this ship will never fly!'

In response, the gibbering scientist hit the ship's ignition switch and threw the throttles wide open. Jerkov's craft leapt into the sky and roared, at terrifying speed, in the direction of Los Angeles.

'Dong!' Deadman threw himself out of the cab and waved his arms. 'Dong! Come down! I know you're upset, but we can fix this! Come down, baby! Come to poppa!'

For a moment, Dong stared down blearily at his mentor and appeared to consider. But then he looked up as a multi-engined airliner roared overhead. Some sixth sense told the great ape that this was the plane that was carrying his lost love forever beyond his reach.

Tears pouring down his face, the gigantic beast spread his arms in a last, hopeless, beseeching gesture. 'Raaaaaaaaaayyyyyyyyyyyyyyyy!'

A second cab arrived. Ann Darling stepped out and stood, hands on hips, glaring up at her errant husband.

'Dong! What are you doin' foolin' about up there? You'd better come down here right this minute, Mister!'

Dong cringed before his spouse's wrath. In his distraction he failed to notice the rocket-propelled menace that came, roaring, from the desert.

In the cabin of the uncontrollable ship, Jerkov and his reluctant co-pilot stared at the doom that was about to befall them.

'What is that?' shrieked Jerkov. 'Is it a moon of Venus?'

'No,' said his companion, closing his eyes. 'I believe it is the incredibly huge ass of a thirty-foot gorilla.'

The ship executed a high-speed docking manoeuvre between Dong's mountainous buttocks.

'Raaaaaaaaa – uh?!' Dong swayed. His eyes crossed. Something that might have been an incredulous grin, or a rictus of agony, swept across his face. He tried to regain his balance, but he was fighting his biological make-up and gravity.

The great ape gave a heart-rending groan and toppled forwards.

Far below, Deadman stared up, his face twisted into a mask of terror. 'Dong! Noooooooooooo!'

Dong fell, demolishing the sign and symbol of

Tinseltown in his final agonies, and landed on top of Deadman with an earth-shaking crash.

A large crowd gathered to view the remains.

'What happened?' demanded a rubber-necker. 'Did the airplanes get him?'

Indiana held his disreputable hat over his heart in an attitude of respect. He glanced at Ann. 'No, it wasn't the airplanes,' he intoned. 'It was Beauty killed the Beast.'

'If you say so,' said Ann. 'Frankly, I think being hit in the butt by a hundred-ton spaceship didn't help.'

'Well, I guess that's that.' Indiana sighed and turned away. 'What will you do now?'

'I dunno.' Ann fell into step beside him. 'Selznick asked me to play some woman called Scarlett something – I mean, is he kidding? What kind of a name is Scarlett? – in some Civil War movie with Gable, *Gone Up in Smoke* or whatever the hell it's called.' Ann shrugged. 'Anyhow, I'm gonna turn it down, it sounds like a turkey. How about you?'

Indiana put his hat back on his head and adjusted the brim. 'I had a call from some guy here, says he wants to make some movies about my life. I said I'd talk to him, but I don't get it. Why would anyone want to see a movie about an archaeologist?'

Ann curled her lip. 'I can't imagine.'

Away to the west, the sky blazed in the sunset.

Arm in arm, they walked into it.

Epilogue

Back on Skullandcrossbones Island, the sun was rising. Mist covered the jungle floor as the creatures of the island began to wake.

In the trees, birds squawked and squeaked. Leaves trembled from the heavy thudding of animals rising from their slumbers.

Amidst the noise of the jungle an incessant thump of footsteps could be heard accompanied by a faint plaintive cry.

'Daaaaaaaaad!'

From out of the mist the figure of an ape emerged.

'Daaaaaad!'

The hairy beast ambled through the undergrowth, his front paws dragging along the ground.

'Daaaaaaad!'

The creature bore more than a passing resemblance to a recent past inhabitant of the island. Swinging between its legs was a prodigious bodily part.

Like father, like son ...